Should you read this book? To find out, read the following ten statements and mark whether or not they are true.

- I have suffered a heart attack — Yes/No
- I have high blood pressure — Yes/No
- I worry that stress is harming my health — Yes/No
- I am quick to anger — Yes/No
- I constantly race to meet deadlines — Yes/No
- I strive hard to succeed in life — Yes/No
- I am more ambitious than most — Yes/No
- I find it hard to trust people — Yes/No
- I have a cynical outlook — Yes/No
- I feel tense much of the time — Yes/No

A *yes* to any one of these statements and this book should be essential reading.

If you have already suffered a heart attack, the programme described will help speed your return to a full, active and healthful lifestyle.

If stressful living is causing you concern, the same programme could bring you back from the brink of a heart attack.

OTHER TITLES IN THIS SERIES:

Agoraphobia
Angina
Asthma
Back Pain
Banish Anxiety
Beat Psoriasis
Bulimia
Coming Off Tranquillizers
Headaches
Herpes Simplex
High Blood Pressure
Hip Replacement
How to Beat Hayfever
Infertility
Low Blood Sugar
ME
Obsessive Compulsive Disorder
Overcoming Depression
Overcoming Incontinence
Panic Attacks
Post-Traumatic Stress Disorder
Prostate Problems
RSI
SAD
Schizophrenia
Stress
Super Potency
Tinnitus
Understanding Paranoia

HEART ATTACK

HOW TO RETURN TO A FULL, HEALTHY AND ACTIVE LIFESTYLE

*Dr David Lewis
and Dr John Storey*

Thorsons
An Imprint of HarperCollins*Publishers*

Thorsons
An Imprint of HarperCollins*Publishers*
77–85 Fulham Palace Road
Hammersmith, London W6 8JB
1160 Battery Street
San Francisco, California 94111–1213

Published by Thorsons 1990
This edition 1995
9 7 5 3 1 10 8 6 4 2

© David Lewis and John Storey 1990

David Lewis and John Storey assert the moral right to
be identified as the authors of this work

A catalogue record for this book
is available from the British Library

ISBN 0 7225 3227 X

Typeset by Harper Phototypesetters Limited
Northampton, England
Printed in Great Britain by
HarperCollinsManufacturing Glasgow

All rights reserved. No part of this publication may be
reproduced, stored in a retrieval system, or transmitted,
in any form or by any means, electronic, mechanical,
photocopying, recording or otherwise, without the prior
permission of the publishers.

CONTENTS

Introduction vii

1 Your Journey Back 1
2 Your Vulnerable Heart 13
3 Assessing Your Risk Factors 26
4 Personality and Heart Disease 55
5 Heart and Mind 67
6 Creative Stress Management 80
7 Developing Awareness 93
8 Change Your Mind – To Save Your Heart 111
9 The Relaxation Response 134
10 Food for a Healthy Heart 170
11 Plan-21 – Your Key to a Healthy Heart 194
12 Exercise for a Healthy Heart 209

Index 223

INTRODUCTION

This is a practical book designed to help two sorts of reader. First there are those who have suffered a heart attack and seek guidance on how to return to a normal, active lifestyle.

Second are people who worry that their fast-paced, high pressure way of life may be putting them at risk of heart disease. Perhaps you have been warned by your GP to slow down and take life more easily. The problem is that, as with much sound advice, it is easier to agree with than to put into practice!

What can, and should, you do to come back from the reality or the risk of heart disease? This book provides the answers. The information we give can be divided into two kinds: the *Why* and the *How*.

We explain *why* certain activities or attitudes are harmful in order to establish the medical and psychological basis for our advice. Many of you will be interested and wish to read this. Others, however, may be prepared to take what we say on trust and prefer to go straight to the practicalities of bringing about positive health-promoting changes in their lifestyle.

To meet the needs of both types of reader we have, so far

as is possible, separated background facts from practical procedures. The latter are keyed as 'Action Chapters'. In them you will find the nitty-gritty of what should be done with only a minimum of additional comment, explanation or illustration.

A heart attack is a highly stressful event and, it you have recently suffered one, your mood is likely to be one of great apprehension, uncertainty and perhaps resentment. These are understandable and common reactions which we shall explore further in the first chapter. For the moment let us just offer this reassurance. The way back from a heart attack may not always be smooth or easy, but it is a journey you can certainly make with knowledge and persistence. In this book we shall provide that essential information. The persistence must come from you. Good luck and have a successful journey.

1

YOUR JOURNEY BACK

When 42-year-old Martin suffered and survived a serious heart attack his immediate reaction was anger – 'Why me?' Then came an overwhelming sensation of guilt: 'How could I put my family through this?' Finally intense anxiety: 'Is it going to happen again?'

Your interest in this book suggests that either you, or a loved one, have recently been through a similar, highly stressful experience. If so, your responses could well have been similar to Martin's. Anger, guilt, anxiety and worry are commonplace and raise important questions in the minds of both sufferers and their families:

- 'How far can I trust my body again?'
- 'Will life ever be the same?'
- 'What can I do to protect my health from now on?'
- 'How much exercise is it safe to take?'
- 'What types of activities must be avoided?'
- 'Must I change my diet?'

Hopefully you will have a sympathetic GP who will be able to provide answers to some of your queries. But this is by no means certain. A recent survey suggested that of the more than 120,000 British and 700,000 American patients who leave hospital each year after a heart attack, only a small minority receive adequate guidance or satisfactory practical advice about returning to health. All too often they are left to their own devices, to gain what knowledge and advice they can from magazines, relatives or fellow sufferers. As a result, not surprisingly, they suffer confusion and anxiety, their confidence is shaken and their self-esteem undermined.

Our book is a practical guide to that journey back to health and happiness. We offer an easily implemented programme of change that will help you achieve a new lifestyle, in many ways richer and more fulfilling than your old.

If you have not suffered an attack, but are concerned that your way of life is increasing the risk of one, this same approach can safeguard your health while enhancing your well-being.

Martin, who made the trip from coronary care to full health a couple of years ago, regards his heart attack not as the end but the start of everything. Remarkably he considers it one of the most rewarding experiences of his life.

Martin's Journey Back

'Looking at my lifestyle before the attack I now realize I was a textbook case,' Martin admits. 'Yet when the attack came it took me completely by surprise. I remember thinking, "This is ridiculous. I'm far too young . . . it can't be happening to me."'

At the time of his attack Martin, who owned a chain of successful DIY shops, was a 60lbs overweight, 40 cigarettes a day workaholic. He took little exercise and drove nearly

80,000 miles each year, much of it through heavy traffic, on inspection tours of his branches. He drank a lot and ate several business lunches each week.

At a medical a few weeks prior to his attack, his blood pressure had been 180 over 95 (these figures are explained in the next chapter) and his resting pulse was 75 beats per minute. After only a few minutes' brisk exercise, however, this increased to 165 and the slightest exertion left him breathless.

His blood cholesterol was 7.4mmol/litre (286mg/100ml) and his triglyceride level was 2.8mmol/litre (248mg/100ml). His blood uric level was raised but his blood glucose was normal. We'll be explaining the significance of these medical findings later in the book.

There were, however, no objective signs of heart disease apart from the high blood pressure which is, unfortunately, all too common in our society. Martin's smoking, hypertension (high blood pressure) and raised cholesterol level (anything above 5.2mmol/litre (200mg/100ml) is a threat) had nonetheless created an eight-fold increase in the risk of coronary heart disease. As Martin now admits: 'I was a heart attack looking for somewhere to happen.'

Yet in recounting this litany of physical excesses, Martin never mentioned what was – in our view – perhaps the most serious health risk of all. This was his generally hostile and untrusting attitude towards others which led to fierce arguments and violent rages. Martin defends this outlook by pointing out he needed all the toughness he could muster in order to create a million-pound business from humble beginnings:

> *You can't do that by letting people walk all over you; trusting people too much; by being all sweetness and light. My reputa-*

tion was as a hard man. Not the kind you'd willingly do down or get on the wrong side of. Somebody who wasn't afraid to say what he thought, or lose his temper when the situation demanded it.

On the day of his attack, Martin was exhausted after a trip to New York, which included five hours delayed at Kennedy airport. During the journey he had eaten well and had a fair amount to drink. Arriving at Heathrow, tired out and in a furious temper, he was forced to hang around for another 30 minutes until the company car arrived. 'When the driver finally turned up I blew my top,' Martin recalls. 'All the anger and frustrations of the previous 12 hours were aimed at my unfortunate chauffeur.'

The next thing Martin knew was an increasingly severe pain in his chest and throat:

I felt as if I was choking. At the same time came a crushing feeling spreading from my chest and down my left arm. My first thought was indigestion, but instead of going away the pain just got worse and worse.

Martin was experiencing the classical symptoms of a heart attack.

Prompt medical attention saved his life and six weeks later, after making a good recovery, he was back at work. 'Apart from being told to take things easily and give up smoking, I received no advice or guidance,' he says.

Martin set about rebuilding his life with the same determination and resourcefulness which had made him so successful in business. He read everything he could find on diet and exercise:

I read an article which said walking was as healthy as jogging and thought, even in my state of health, I should be capable of going for a walk. But I was very apprehensive. The heart attack had given my confidence a real hammering and I felt extremely wary about risking any sort of exertion. So I decided to build my health up slowly, set realistic goals and keep written notes to guide my progress. I measured a route from my home to a nearby park which was just over a mile and made up my mind to walk it every day no matter what the weather. The first time it took me 30 minutes and I was sweating at the end.

I changed my eating habits, reducing generally and cutting out red meat. I managed to stop smoking. It wasn't as hard as I expected.

All these beneficial changes helped reduce the risk of Martin becoming one of a significant number of patients who suffer a second heart attack within 12 months of the first.

But no less crucial than these physical changes was Martin's decision to do something about his anger. 'I knew enough to know it had nearly killed me once,' he explained, 'and could still send me to an early grave.'

Changing his outlook to become more trusting and less hostile was no easy task. But Martin achieved it by learning from one of the present authors (David Lewis) procedures for bringing even powerful emotions under control.

Today, two years later, Martin's weight is down from 210 to 154lbs – correct for his height – his blood pressure is normally at 130 over 80, and his blood cholesterol is lower than that found in most men of his age. He has a brisk five-mile walk each day without the slightest feelings of discomfort and his resting pulse is down from 75 to 55.

'When I meet people who haven't seen me since before the attack they often don't recognize me,' he says cheerfully.

'I look so slim and feel so healthy. It's like being a 20-year-old all over again.'

Equally impressive is Martin's new outlook on life. He still works hard and is very much in charge of his company, but the former hostility and the temper which led to so many bitter rows have gone for good:

> *Without caring any less, I am now able to adopt a much more laid-back approach to problems and frustrations. I no longer react with such anger when things go wrong. In fact I now realize that many of those problems and set-backs were self-inflicted – the result of how I responded to difficult situations and dealt with other people.*

Martin regards his present relaxed, healthy lifestyle as something of a miracle. Yet his achievements are capable of being duplicated by virtually every heart attack victim. For them, too, this experience could prove the start of a new and even richer life, rather than the collapse of all their hopes and dreams.

But, sadly, instead of being the beginning of a rewarding journey back to health and happiness, an attack is often seen as the end of everything. The end of ambition at work. The end of contentment at home. The end of achievements. The end of sexual activity. The end of self-confidence. The end of self-esteem.

Why should this be? Why do heart attack victims like Martin tend to be an exception rather than the rule?

Sometimes, of course, the barriers on the journey are medical. Where serious damage has been done to the heart, returning to an entirely normal life may prove impossible. Even in the most serious cases, however, a considerable degree of recovery can be achieved.

This barrier may be one of ignorance. The sufferer simply

does not know how to make the journey back or maybe does not even realize that such a return trip is possible. Martin had to invest a great deal of time and effort in finding out how to recover his health. You will find all that essential information between the covers of this book.

But just as often the major roadblocks on the way back to full health are psychological barriers.

Before describing what these barriers are, we suggest you take the following test. Do this by scoring each statement as follows: very true = 3; true to some extent = 2; not true at all = 1.

SELF-ASSESSMENT	Score
1 I put off difficult decisions to the last minute.	
2 I would sooner not be told bad news.	
3 I believe most of my problems are caused by other people.	
4 I prefer to avoid awkward confrontations.	
5 I would sooner not know about cruelty and injustices.	
6 I am frequently let down by others.	
7 I delegate unpleasant tasks whenever possible.	
8 I think luck plays a big part in success.	
9 I feel some people dislike me for no good reason.	
10 I would sooner complain about poor service or shoddy goods by letter than in person.	
11 I believe most people are kind and good.	
12 I have often been the victim of other people's incompetence.	
Total	

Score
12–15: average score; 16–28 moderately high score; 29–36: high score

WHAT YOUR SCORES REVEAL
This assessment explored your response to the three main ways in which we defend ourselves against anxiety.

If your score for the four statements relating to each of these defence mechanisms is greater than 6, it suggests this strategy is used too frequently.

Strategy 1 – Avoidance
Explored in statements 1;4;7;10.

Strategy 2 – Denial of reality
Explored in statements 2;5;8;11.

Strategy 3 – Projection
Explored in statements 3;6;9;12.

What These Strategies Involve

AVOIDANCE
It is only natural to avoid something you know will be unpleasant or distressing. In moderation this is a perfectly sensible way of making life more bearable. After all, deliberately exposing oneself to stressful events would be very demoralizing.

But there are two main reasons why avoidance is usually an ineffective, even hazardous, way of coping with anxiety.

First, it reduces the possibility of being able to confront that situation in the future. This is how phobias – an intense fear, considered irrational because whatever arouses it is not objectively dangerous – arise. A person sees or hears something which, for various reasons, arouses anxiety. This produces either distressing physical symptoms (such as a rapidly beating heart, 'butterflies in the stomach', dry mouth, increased sweating and so on) or fearful and handicapping thoughts: 'I can't cope . . . I must escape . . . I am going to faint.' On many occasions both physical and mental symptoms are present.

Avoiding whatever has aroused the anxiety quickly reduces the distressing symptoms. A child afraid of a maths lesson, for instance, soon feels calm again if his mother agrees to his missing class that day. That reduction in anxiety rewards the avoidance, making it more likely on the next occasion. Psychologists call this 'law of effect'. It simply means that, as common sense suggests, we are more inclined to do rewarding than punishing things. After a while, however, the anxiety and avoidance can spread. A child who starts out fearful of maths and avoids those lessons by playing truant, for instance, may end up afraid of all his classes and finally of the school itself.

The second point is that whenever we avoid something important, vital lessons fail to be learned. Take somebody with a social phobia. This common fear leads to party invitations being refused and makes friendships difficult to form. The result is that the skills needed to make friends and get along with others in a relaxed setting are never mastered. Even when this fear is overcome the individual may still feel awkward and lack confidence in social encounters.

What has all this to do with coming back from a heart attack?

Research, and the experience of many health professionals, suggests victims of heart attacks are often reluctant to confront the health issues involved.

This was the experience of 67-year-old Geoff Whitten who, following his own heart attack in 1976, set up a self-help group to assist fellow victims to cope with their fears and avoid the isolation he experienced.

His local hospital distributed leaflets inviting patients to contact him. Many GPs also urged their heart patients to get in touch. Not a single one did so. Doctors attributed this lack of response, in part, to avoidance and a fear of talking openly about a life-threatening event.

Instead of confronting the fact that they have suffered an attack, a majority of victims would sooner not even think about it. They are one of the few groups of people with a serious health problem who do not have their own self-help network.

Geoff Whitten, incidentally, developed his own fitness programme, involving first walking, then swimming and cycling. Today he cycles around 3,000 miles each year, is physically fitter than in his fifties and considers his life has changed for the better since the attack.

Avoidance such as has been described is a major barrier to recovery. For unless and until a person accepts he or she has a heart problem, the journey back cannot even begin. If your score on statements 1,4,7 and 10 was 6 or more, consider whether you are facing up to the situation realistically.

If you are the partner of a heart patient, this book may have been bought in an attempt to persuade him or her to accept the situation. Continue exerting reasonable pressure to face up to the situation, and emphasize that far from coming to terms with being a semi-invalid, such acceptance means voting for a long and healthy life.

DENIAL OF REALITY
When given bad news our instinctive response is to gasp 'Oh, no . . .' and deny the reality of what we have just been

told. As with avoidance, such denial is not necessarily a bad thing.

An elderly woman who denies the reality of her spouse's death, perhaps even to the extent of continuing to set a place for him at meals, may be sustained in her grief by this strategy. A young woman who adopted the same approach, however, would be denying herself the opportunity to rebuild her life.

Denying the reality of an attack and insisting, as some sufferers do, 'I am not even going to think about what happened to me,' makes it impossible to bring about urgently needed changes in lifestyle and attitude. Note the important difference between avoidance and denial.

When *avoiding* something we tell ourselves: 'I know I should be doing that, it's relevant and important to me, but I can't face it.' In *denial* we say: 'There is no reason why I should be doing that, it's not relevant or important to me.'

A score of 6 or more on statements 2, 5, 8 and 11 suggests you rely too greatly on denial of reality for dealing with anxiety.

PROJECTION

This takes the form of projecting one's powerful emotions — anger guilt, frustration, etc. — onto other people. When this strategy was described to Martin, he immediately admitted having used it after his heart attack:

I blamed everybody but myself. I practically accused my wretched driver of trying to kill me. I blamed my family for demanding too much, my wife for not being sufficiently understanding, my fellow directors for putting me under too much pressure . . . I even blamed the airline for delaying the flight.

So long as one searches for scapegoats and uses projection to cope with the intense anxiety a heart attack arouses, so long will progress towards health be delayed.

If you scored 6 or more on statements 3, 6, 9 and 12, consider the extent to which you might be using projection to avoid dealing directly with anxiety-arousing ideas and issues. Should you be the partner of a patient, do not feel surprised – or too hurt – if you sometimes seem to be blamed either for what happened or for the slow progress towards better health. Tactfully but firmly direct your partner's attention to his or her central role in recovery.

A high overall score on this assessment (29–36) indicates that all three strategies are being employed to help you defend yourself against the anxiety which having suffered a heart attack naturally arouses.

If your score was even moderately high, then at least two of these strategies are likely to be used from time to time. In either case we urge you to reflect on what we've written and consider, as objectively as possible, the extent to which you may be creating needless barriers to enjoying a full and healthy lifestyle.

The motto of the Parachute Regiment – 'Knowledge Conquers Fear' – could well apply to many medical conditions. Knowing what has happened to you, and why, can greatly reduce apprehension and anxiety.

In one study it was found that patients given detailed and accurate information about the type and extent of post-operative pain found their recovery significantly less painful and distressing than patients denied such knowledge. With this in mind, the next chapter will explain how and why heart disease occurs.

2

YOUR VULNERABLE HEART

Form your hand into a fist, and you will have a fair idea of the size of the remarkable pump on which your life depends. Despite its modest dimensions, the human heart is an astonishingly robust and powerful organ. During the average lifetime it beats more than three billion times, each week pumping some seven tons of blood – sufficient to fill Concorde's fuel tanks – around thousands of miles of arteries, veins and capillaries in the circulatory system.

Yet, while resilient and reliable, your heart is also vulnerable. What places it at risk are not the extremes of inadequate diet and insufficient exercise found in excessively unhealthy lifestyles, but the factors present in the way most of us live. Before considering why this should be so, let's take a brief look at the way your heart works in order to understand what can go wrong and why.

Your Hard-Working Heart

LOCATION
The heart, enclosed in a double-walled sac called the *pericardium*, and surrounded by the lungs, is located on

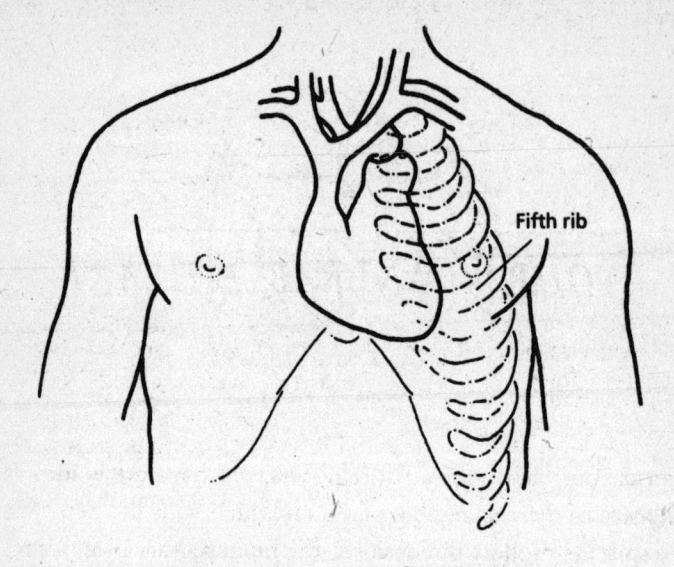

Figure 1 The location of your heart.

the front and centre of a sheet of muscle (the *diaphragm*) which separates the chest and abdominal cavities. A healthy heart occupies less than 50 per cent of the diameter of the chest cavity (the *cardiothoracic ratio (CTR)*) with the tip of the left ventricle touching the chest wall, four inches to the left of the breastbone, between the fourth and fifth ribs.

Each time the heart contracts a pulsation can be felt at the apex point – the *apex beat*. If a heart is abnormally enlarged, this beat is displayed outward and downward so that it is felt below the fifth rib.

FUNCTION
The heart pumps a constant supply of purplish, deoxygenated blood to the lungs and bright red, oxygenated blood to the rest of the body. This is achieved by means of four

Left heart: Receives oxygen-rich blood from the lungs and pumps it through the aorta to the body.

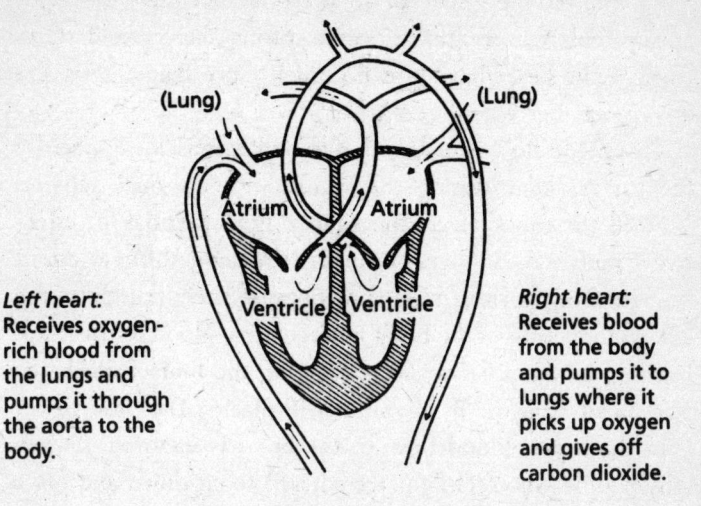

Right heart: Receives blood from the body and pumps it to lungs where it picks up oxygen and gives off carbon dioxide.

Figure 2 How your heart works.

chambers, two on each side of the heart, separated by a wall of tissue called the *septum*. Between each pair of chambers there is a valve, the *tricuspid* on the right side and the *bicuspid*, or *mitral* – so called because early anatomists were struck by the resemblance to a bishop's mitre – on the left. A malfunction of these valves can usually be detected by sounds your doctor hears when listening through a stethoscope.

Heart beats are triggered by electrical signals generated in a collection of cells, called the *sinoatrial node* or pacemaker.

At any time the heart may be in one of two conditions: *diastole* (relaxed) or *systole* (contracted). As we shall explain in the next chapter, these are the two measures made when blood pressure is taken.

In the relaxed state, blood flows into the top right chamber (the atrium) via two large veins, the superior and inferior *venae cave*. From there it passes into the lower (ventricle) chamber through the tricuspid valve.

Around 80 per cent of blood flow between the right atrium and right ventricle occurs during this relaxed state, without the heart having to do much more than top up the lower chamber when it contracts.

This blood flow is mainly due to bodily muscles, especially the calves, compressing the veins during normal activity. Termed the *muscle pump*, this squeezing is essential for effective circulation. Soldiers compelled to stand stiffly at attention for long periods may faint because their muscle pump can no longer assist the heart in circulating blood to the head. Fainting is nature's way of preventing the brain from being starved of oxygen. By involuntarily placing the head lower than the heart, blood flow to the brain is restored. This is why people who feel faint are advised to sit down and place their head between their knees. Should you ever have to stand or sit for long periods, say, while making a long flight, be sure to get up and move around several times each hour in order to keep the muscle pump working.

An electrical wave of about 2.4 volts causes the atrium to contract, sending a small amount of additional blood into the ventricle. The wave then spreads to the ventricle, which contracts in turn. As it does so the tricuspid valve snaps shut and pressure inside the chamber increases rapidly. At a certain point the pulmonary valve opens and the blood passes through it, along the pulmonary artery and into the lungs.

There it sheds carbon dioxide and picks up fresh supplies of oxygen before returning to the left atrium through the pulmonary veins. From the atrium it is pumped into the left ventricle. The contraction of this chamber pumps blood through the aorta on its long journey to transport food and oxygen to every cell in the body.

The heart too receives oxygen-rich blood through the right and left coronary arteries leading off the aorta.

When the oxygen has been extracted, this blood returns to the right atrium via the coronary vein. As with every bodily tissue the heart muscle must have a constant supply of oxygen-rich blood. If deprived of blood, death of muscle tissue will occur. This is what happens during a heart attack, known medically as a *myocardial infarction*.

REGULATING THE PUMP

Although heart beats are automatic, triggered by the pacemaker cells, the rate of pumping can be modified by two sets of nerves, the *vagus* and the *sympathetic*, in order to cope with changing demands. The vagus slows the heart, while the sympathetic nerve speeds its action. During exercise or if you become emotionally aroused the sympathetic nerve increases heart rate as part of an arousal mechanism whose effects we describe later in the book.

WARNING SIGNS

There are many different types of heart disease but in this book we focus on the most common and tragic – coronary heart disease (CHD).

CHD never comes out of the blue. There are always warning signs. All too often, however, these are either ignored or confused with something else, such as indigestion. As cardiac function deteriorates, physical and mental performance declines. The patient spends more and more time accomplishing less and less. After a while even the simplest task becomes beyond him. This increases the pressures at work as schedules are thrown into confusion, deadlines missed and chaos reigns.

In some instances such warnings reveal a defective oxygen supply to the tissues which becomes apparent as demands on the heart increase, for instance during vigorous exercise or strong emotions. These may trigger an attack of *angina pectoris* — the name comes from two Latin words meaning 'pain in the chest' — experienced as a severe, constricting pain that typically radiates to the left shoulder and down the left arm.

Angina is caused by a narrowing of the arteries which supply blood to the heart. This may be due to a furring up of the vessels (*atheroma*, from the Greek meaning 'porridge') and/or a spasm of the arteries. A heart attack is caused by a blockage in one of the coronary arteries which causes the supply of blood to part of the heart muscle to be cut off. This is usually due to the formation of a clot of blood (a *thrombosis*) in an artery already damaged by fatty atheroma. If the damage to heart muscle is sufficiently severe the heart may stop beating entirely — a *cardiac arrest*.

There is severe pain, which usually lasts for several hours, from the oxygen-starved muscle, and the victim also usually feels faint, giddy or sick.

Coronary heart disease is now the Western world's major killer, accounting for nearly a third of deaths from all causes. In the time it has taken you to read this far in the chapter at least two people will have collapsed and died in the UK as a result of CHD. In many cases these deaths could have been prevented by making changes in outlook, attitudes and lifestyle. It is with these heart-saving changes that our book is concerned.

YOU ARE AS YOUNG AS YOUR ARTERIES
'The rule of the artery is supreme,' wrote Dr Andrew Still in the 1800s, and his message remains as true and as timely a century later. The key to health and vigour is an efficient circulatory system.

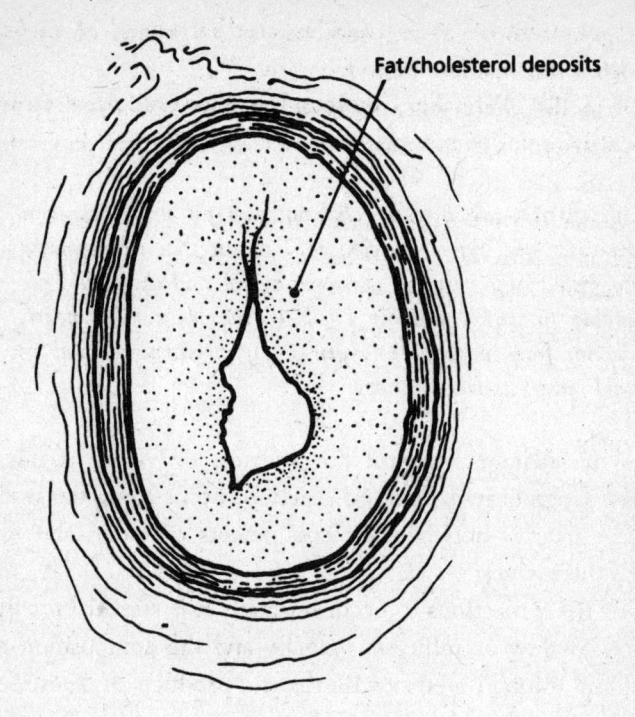

Figure 3 *Section of coronary artery showing narrowing due to deposits of fat and cholesterol.*

When young, our arteries are clean, smooth-walled and extremely flexible. They meet varying demands for blood, including sudden surges in demand, by rapidly dilating or constricting.

But, as we age, our way of life takes a relentless toll. The arteries become as encrusted, thick and brittle as a length of old hosepipe left to rot in the sun. As early as our twentieth birthday we may possess the arterial system of a person 40 years older. During the Korean war, army surgeons performing routine autopsies on American servicemen in their late teens and twenties were horrified to find atheroma in 95 per cent of cases. Decades later surgeons in Vietnam reported identical findings.

Dr Julian Whitaker, director of the California Heart Medical Clinic, comments:

> Our arteries are literally choking with fat and cholesterol deposits. Like a river so clogged with silt that it becomes a sluggish stream, arteries narrowed by fat and cholesterol are unable to carry adequate blood to the heart. The heart, choking from inadequate oxygen supply, begins to die and we have only ourselves to blame.

It is misleading to regard the arteries, or veins, as mere tubes. Complicated chemical reactions occur along the walls of the arteries between the components of blood and the walls themselves.

For these reactions to occur normally it is essential for the blood to flow at sufficient velocity and the composition of the fluid (blood together with the end products of digestion) to remain within the system's functioning capacity. 'You are as old as your arteries,' wrote physician William Osler in 1894. Until comparatively recently his view reflected conventional medical dogma. 'Today,' comments Dr James Julian, 'it is more accurate to say "You are as young as your arteries."' He points out that arteries can be made physiologically younger as well as older by the way we live our lives.

The Signs and Symptoms of Heart Disease

Some CHD patients have a history of angina or have had a previous heart attack; in others the attack comes out of the blue. The severity of an attack varies from mild to very severe. But in some cases there is no pain at all. Doctors have only recently become aware of episodes of *silent ischemia*, during which reduced blood flow starves the heart of oxygen.

In a study which continuously monitored 30 angina patients at London's Hammersmith Hospital, some 2,000 ischemic episodes were recorded, yet pain was felt in less than a quarter of them. Sometimes the psychological defence mechanisms of avoidance and denial, described in the previous chapter, cause patients and/or their spouses to favour a less alarming explanation, such as indigestion or fatigue, for chest pain rather than confronting the more alarming possibility of a heart attack.

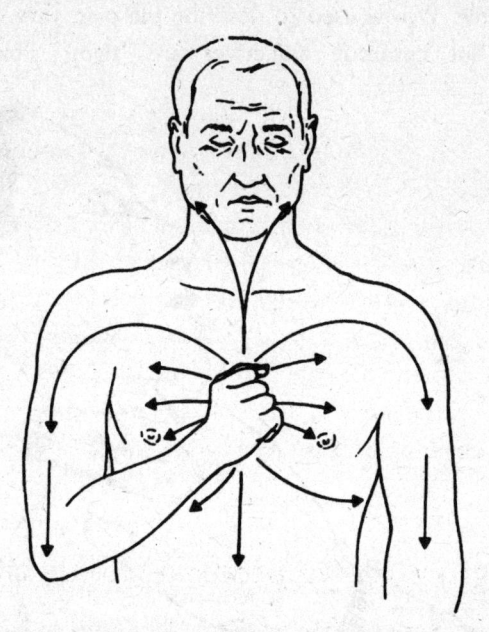

Figure 4 *The site and radiation of cardiac chest pain.*

SYMPTOMS AND SIGNS

The classical symptom of a heart attack is pain in the chest. This has the following characteristics:

- *Location*. The site of the pain is frequently represented by the clenched hand placed on the breastbone.
- *Radiation*. The pain may radiate down the left arm, less often down the right or both arms. It may spread upward into the neck and jaw or downward into the abdomen. In some cases it radiates through to the back or across the chest. To confuse matters further, pain may not be felt in the chest at all, but elsewhere in the body, such as jaw or stomach, so increasing the risk of it being misdiagnosed as toothache or indigestion.
- *Character*. Words used to describe the pain vary considerably, but common adjectives are 'tight', 'band-like',

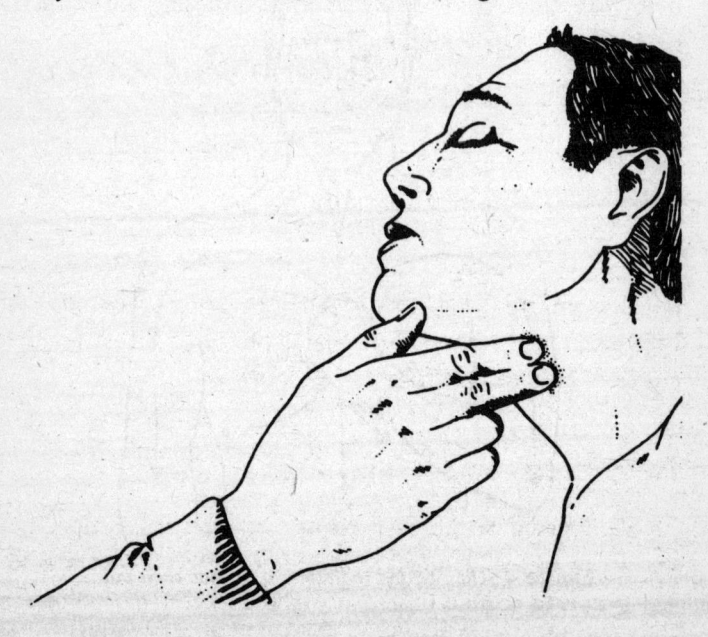

Figure 5 Locating the carotid pulse in the neck.

'oppressive', 'constricting', 'crushing and vice-like', 'weight', 'pressure', 'ache', 'dull', 'squeezing'. When the pain is described as 'stabbing', 'shooting', 'like a needle' or 'knife-like', the cause is not usually heart disease.
- *Duration.* The pain is continuous and not relieved by rest.
- *Associated symptoms.* The patient may be breathless, feel faint or sick.

As well as symptoms (which the patient subjectively reports) there are also signs apparent to trained observers.

- *Appearance.* The victim looks anxious and his colour varies from pale blue to grey. He may be sweating and feel cold.
- *Pulse.* This is usually rapid, but may also be slow and in some cases is irregular.

If you have any doubt always be on the safe side and summon help by calling an ambulance or your doctor.

Cardiac arrest
The most reliable signs of cardiac arrest are a sudden loss of consciousness and the absence of major pulses. The easiest of these to locate is the carotid pulse in the neck, which can be felt by deep pressure either side of the voice box. Additional, but less reliable signs are dilated pupils, the absence of breathing and a grey-blue skin colour. If the heart has stopped, immediate first aid is essential.

Returning to Normal Life

As we stressed in the first chapter, a heart attack does not mean you are condemned to the life of a permanent invalid. The goal is to rebuild fitness slowly and to change anything in your lifestyle which may have contributed to the attack.

SECONDARY PREVENTION

Aimed at preventing a second attack, this includes a reduction of risk factors, the use of drugs, angioplasty and coronary bypass surgery. Angioplasty involves passing a catheter attached to a balloon into the coronary artery, starting either in the leg (femoral artery) or arm (brachial artery).

The surgeon monitors the position of the tip of the catheter using X-rays and, when it arrives at a point where the artery is blocked, inflates the balloon so as to dilate the artery, overcome the obstruction and allow blood to flow more freely.

During a coronary bypass operation, blood is diverted past obstructions in the coronary arteries by transplanting a section of vein taken from the patient's leg. One end is attached to the aorta and the other end positioned just beyond the obstruction.

THE DRUGS YOU MAY BE PRESCRIBED
Beta-Blockers (*brand names: Angilol; Bedranol; Inderal; Sectral; Transicor*)

These drugs are used to lower blood pressure and prevent angina. They are also said to be beneficial in preventing a second attack. The pulse rate is slowed and you may feel tired at first, with cold hands and feet, or experience disturbed sleep.

Glyceryl trinitrate

A small tablet which, placed under the tongue, will quickly relieve the pain of angina by dilating blood vessels and reducing the workload on the left ventricle. Relief lasts up to 30 minutes. Common side-effects are headache and flushing. This drug has recently become available as a patch which you can stick on the skin, allowing the drug to be absorbed slowly over 24 hours.

Calcium antagonists
The two most common are Verapamil (Cordilox) and Nifedipine (Adalat). These affect the chemistry of the heart cells and are used in treating angina and hypertension.

Cholesterol reducing drugs
As we shall see in the next chapter, raised levels of cholesterol in the blood are a risk factor. Where the level is significantly high, drugs may be prescribed to reduce it.

Cholestryramine is the commonest, but the drug is expensive and its side-effects include nausea, constipation or diarrhoea, heartburn, flatulence and stomach pains.

RISK FACTORS
Unfortunately, insufficient attention is usually given to advising patients how to avoid a second attack by reducing avoidable risk factors in their lives. Some hospitals are much better in this respect than others, but all too often the emphasis is on treatment with surgery or medication.

In the next chapter we shall help you explore the major risks present in your lifestyle, while the remainder of the book is concerned with practical procedures for either eliminating or reducing these factors in order to ensure a long, healthy and fulfilling life.

3

ASSESSING YOUR RISK FACTORS

In this chapter we will show you how to assess the extent of risk factors in your lifestyle. These are aspects of your lifestyle or inborn characteristics which inhibit a return to full health following a heart attack or increase the risk of developing coronary heart disease. Your scores will allow you to create a self-help programme tailored to meet your individual requirements.

SCORING THE HEART RISK ASSESSMENT
Complete this assessment by noting down scores associated with your chosen answer. You may wish to write these on a separate sheet to avoid marking the book. This will allow you to monitor progress by completing the assessment on future occasions.

Your Body

1 Strip to the waist and, using thumb and finger, pinch up a fold of skin between waist and hip. Measure the thickness of the fold.

Scoring — Male

(a) Less than ½ inch	No score
(b) ½–1 inch	Score 1
(c) 1–2 inches	Score 2
(d) 2 inches +	Score 3

Scoring — Female

(a) Less than 1 inch	No score
(b) 1–2 inches	Score 1
(c) 2–3 inches	Score 2
(d) 3 inches +	Score 3

2 Carefully measure your waist and hips then compare the two:

(a) Waist less than hips	No score
(b) Waist and hip within ½ inch of each other	Score 1
(c) Waist ½–1 inch greater than hips	Score 2
(d) Waist 1 inch or more than hips	Score 3

3 Weigh yourself undressed. Next calculate your ideal weight as follows:

For men

Multiply your height in inches by 4, then take away 128. For example: for a 5ft 8 inch (68 inch) tall male the calculation is: ideal weight = (68 × 4) − 128 = 144lbs, or 10st 4lbs.

For women

Multiply your height in inches by 3.5 and take away 108. For example: for a 5ft 4 inch (64 inch) tall female the calculation is: ideal weight − (64 × 3.5) − 108=116lbs, or 8st 4lbs.

If your actual weight is:

(a) Within 3lbs of the ideal weight	No score
(b) 4–7lbs above ideal weight	Score 1
(c) 8–14lbs above ideal weight	Score 2
(d) More than 14lbs above ideal weight	Score 3

For the next nine statements you will need a mirror and pocket torch or strong light source.

EXAMINING YOUR MOUTH

4 Compare the edges of your tongue to the illustrations below and notice if they have the 'pie crust' appearance shown in illustration (ii).

How to score
Ignore (a) statements and award 1 point for each (b) ticked.

(a) Normal tongue
(b) Pie crust tongue

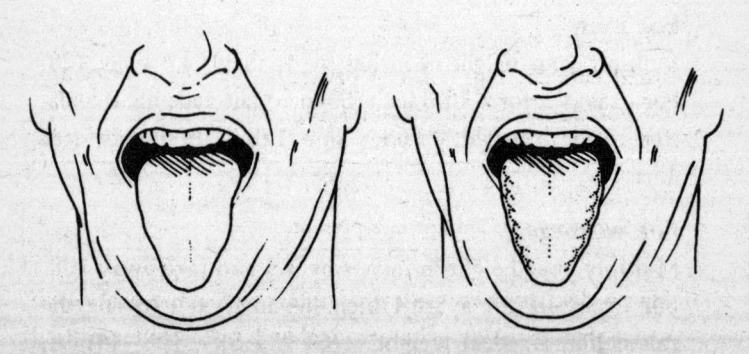

Figure 6 (i) Normal tongue, (ii) 'Pie crust' tongue.

Assessing Your Risk Factors

5 Examine the inside of your cheeks to see whether a white line is present.

   (a) White line absent
   (b) White line present

6 Open and close your mouth in a quiet room and listen carefully for any clicking sounds from the jaw joint.

   (a) Clicking sound absent
   (b) Clicking sound heard

7 Do you notice any stiffness, or restriction of movement, when opening your mouth?

   (a) Jaw moves easily
   (b) Movement feels stiff and restricted

8 Do your jaw muscles feel tender to the touch?

   (a) No tenderness
   (b) Feel tender

9 Check the inside of your cheeks for signs of soreness, small cuts or 'tags' of skin caused by biting or chewing. (A pocket torch may be helpful here.)

   (a) No soreness, cuts or tags seen
   (b) Soreness, cuts and/or tags present

10 Has a dentist ever told you your teeth are worn down more than usual by grinding or clenching – the term used may have been *bruxism*?

(a) Yes
(b) No

11 Do you experience pain at the angle of the jaw or around the temple?

(a) Occasionally
(b) Frequently

12 Do you experience migraine-type headaches?

(a) Rarely or never
(b) Fairly often

Your final score from this part of the assessment is given below.

Number of (b)s ticked	Final score
0–3	No score
4–7	Score 1
8–9	Score 2

Your Cardiovascular System

13 When your blood pressure (BP) is taken, two measures – systolic and diastolic – are obtained. Their meaning will be explained later in this chapter. Here we are concerned only with the higher of the two, the systolic pressure, which reflects your heart's pumping efficiency.

(a) 110–130   No score
(b) 131–149   Score 3
(c) 150–170   Score: aged 35 and below 7; age 36 and above 4
(d) 170+   Score: aged 35 and below 10; age 36 and above 8

As we shall explain later in this chapter, when taken by a doctor your BP may be higher due to the stress involved. BP also varies across time, making it unwise to rely on any single reading. What we are concerned with is chronically *raised BP.*

14 If your cholesterol level has been measured in the last six months use the information in (i) below to score this statement. If you do not know the level refer to (ii) below.

(i) where your cholesterol level is known:

(a) Below 5.2mmol/l (200mg/100ml)	No score
(b) 5.2–6.5mmol/l (200–250mg/100ml)	Score 3
(c) 6.5–7.8mmol/l (251–300mg/100ml)	Score 6
(d) 7.8mmol/l + (301 + mg/100ml)	Score 16

(ii) If you don't know your cholesterol level, score this part of the assessment by awarding +1 point for each of the foods below if you eat them in the quantity given during a typical week.

Food	Quantity per week
Eggs	Two or more
Cheese (except low fat)	More than 5 oz
Milk (exclude skimmed)	More than two pints
Cream	Any amount
Red meat	More than 10 oz
Brains, liver, kidneys	More than 8 oz
Fish roe	Any amount
Sweetbreads	More than 8 oz
Fried foods (not vegetables)	More than twice
Chips	More than twice
Shellfish	More than once
Chocolate	More than 2 oz

Your score depends on the total points:

(a) 0–3 points	No score
(b) 4–6 points	Score 1
(c) 7–15 points	Score 2
(d) 15 + points	Score 4

If you are a diabetic, add a further 10 points to your score.

If you scored (c)s or (d)s on BOTH questions 13 and 14, ADD 50 points to your score.

Diet

15 Salt consumption. This includes salt added to food when cooking or at the table; salty foods (i.e. crisps, salted fish) and convenience foods which are high in salt.
(i) I add salt to my food:

(a) Seldom or never	No score
(b) Fairly often	Score 1
(c) All the time	Score 2

(ii) I eat salty food:

(a) Once a week or less	No score
(b) Twice each week	Score 1
(c) More than twice per week	Score 2

(iii) I eat fast food:

(a) Once a week or less	No score
(b) Twice a week or less	Score 1
(c) More than twice a week	Score 2

16 Your sugar intake can be estimated by counting the number of portions eaten on a normal day. A portion consists of the following amounts:

Sweets, chocolates, jam, honey	per ounce
Sugar in drinks, i.e. tea or coffee	per teaspoon
Soft drinks (except slimmer's)	per glass
Cakes, puddings, biscuits	per helping
Breakfast cereals with sugar	per serving
Canned vegetables	per serving

(a) 0–2	No score
(b) 3–4	Score 3
(c) 5–6	Score 4
(d) 6+	Score 5

17 Alcohol is measured in Standard Units. One unit equals half a pint of beer, lager, cider, etc. or one glass of wine, sherry or vermouth, or one measure (⅙ gill) spirits. For example, three pints of beer = 6 Standard Units. Total your average consumption *in units* per day.

Units consumed	Final score
(a) 0–1	No score
(b) 2–3	1
(c) 4–5	3
(d) 6 +	4

18 Award one point for the number of portions of fresh vegetables, fruit, bran, pulses and wholemeal bread eaten in an average week. A portion consists of the following:

Fresh fruit	Per item
Fresh (raw) vegetables	8 oz
Bran, pulses and other high roughage foods	4 oz
Wholemeal bread	per slice

Total points	Final score
(a) More than 10 points	No score
(b) 7–9	1
(c) 4–6	2
(d) Fewer than 4	3

19 Do you live in a hard water area?

(a) Yes	No score
(b) No	Score 1

Family Health History

20 These statements are concerned with the number of parents, brothers or sisters who suffer from or — if deceased — suffered from heart disease.

(a) No history of heart disease	Deduct 10 points from your score total
(b) One parent or sibling over 60 with heart trouble	No score
(c) Both parents or siblings over 60 with heart trouble	Score 2
(d) One parent or sibling under 60 with heart trouble	Score 5
(e) Both parents or siblings under 60 with heart trouble	Score 10

Smoking

21 If you have been a non-smoker for more than seven years *deduct* 5 points from your total score. If you smoked cigarettes up to the time of your attack (or are continuing to smoke) score as follows:

(a) Up to 20 cigarettes per day	Score 5
(b) 20–40 per day	Score 10
(c) 40 + per day	Score 15

If you smoked (or smoke) a pipe a day or two cigars per week, score 2.

If you smoke more than one pipe a day or two cigars per week, score 3.

Exercise

22 Prior to your heart attack (or at the present time if you have not suffered an attack) did you/do you take at least 20 minutes' brisk exercise (i.e. sufficient to raise your pulse rate and make you sweat):

> IF YOU HAVE SUFFERED A HEART ATTACK YOU SHOULD NOT UNDERTAKE SUCH EXERCISE WITHOUT TAKING MEDICAL ADVICE!

(a) Five times per week	*Deduct* 5 from your total score
(b) 3–4 times per week	*Deduct* 3 from your total score
(c) 1–2 times per week	*Deduct* 1 from your total score
(d) Less than once a week	*Add* 3 to your total score

Emotions

23 Choose the statements which reflect your behaviour on most occasions.

When talking I . . .

- repeat words for emphasis
- 'spit out' the first words of sentences
- talk fast
- speak loudly
- answer questions quickly
- reply before the other speaker has finished
- interrupt others
- finish other people's sentences for them
- respond to attempts to interrupt me by talking more loudly
- become impatient with people who speak slowly

Assessing Your Risk Factors 37

Add 2 points to your score for each statement ticked.

Note
The remaining statements are scored as follows: (a) no score (b) 2 (c) 3.

24 I become angry and impatient when stuck in traffic jams. (a) Not true at all (b) True to some extent (c) Very true.
25 I get very irritated if served by a slow shop assistant. (a) Not true at all (b) True to some extent (c) Very true.
26 I hate waiting in a queue. (a) Not true at all (b) True to some extent (c) Very true.
27 I try and do a great many things at once. (a) Not true at all (b) True to some extent (c) Very true.
28 I often go over the speed limit when driving. (a) Not true at all (b) True to some extent (c) Very true.
29 I like beating other motorists away from traffic lights. (a) Not true at all (b) True to some extent (c) Very true.
30 I fear life will be too short to accomplish all I wish. (a) Not true at all (b) True to some extent (c) Very true.
31 I am very ambitious. (a) Not true at all (b) True to some extent (c) Very true.
32 I have a strong desire to win at almost any cost. (a) Not true at all (b) True to some extent (c) Very true.
33 I like working to deadlines. (a) Not true at all (b) True to some extent (c) Very true.
34 I have difficulty telling someone I love them. (a) Not true at all (b) True to some extent (c) Very true.
35 I hide my true feelings. (a) Not true at all (b) True to some extent (c) Very true.
36 I am embarrassed by open displays of emotion. (a) Not true at all (b) True to some extent (c) Very true.
37 I believe that, given the opportunity, most people will

cheat or deceive you. (a) Not true at all (b) True to some extent (c) Very true.
38. I seldom fully trust people. (a) Not true at all (b) True to some extent (c) Very true.
39. I have a quick temper. (a) Not true at all (b) True to some extent (c) Very true.
40. I become angry over minor set-backs or frustrations. (a) Not true at all (b) True to some extent (c) Very true.
41. I tend to blame others when things go wrong. (a) Not true at all (b) True to some extent (c) Very true.
42. I have difficulty laughing at myself. (a) Not true at all (b) True to some extent (c) Very true.
43. I deal with aggressive people as part of my regular work. (a) Not true at all (b) True to some extent (c) Very true.
44. I resent people less able than myself achieving more than I do. (a) Not true at all (b) True to some extent (c) Very true.
45. I feel life has been unfair to me. (a) Not true at all (b) True to some extent (c) Very true.

What Your Score Reveals

The higher the score, the greater your risk of suffering a further, or first, heart attack. To gain a general impression of the risk factors present in your current lifestyle fill in the chart opposite. Block out one oblong for each point.

You might like to copy or photocopy this score target so as to repeat the assessment on future occasions.

The closer you are to the centre of the chart – which represents an artery being gradually clogged by atheroma – the greater the threat to your health.

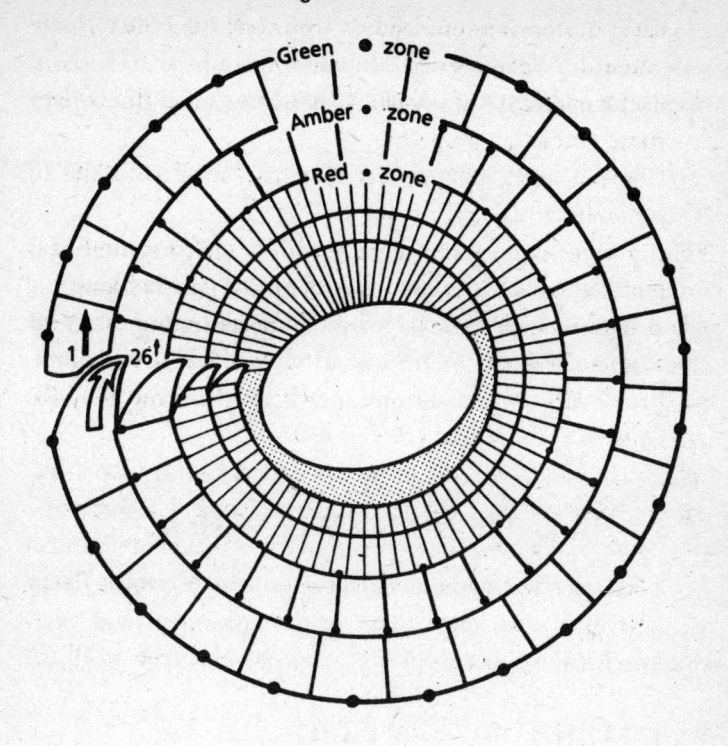

Figure 7 The risk chart.

GREEN ZONE

If you remain in this zone the overall risk level is low and you are to be congratulated on taking such sensible care of your health. Even with a green total, however, it is still possible that your score for one or more of the 10 risk factors was too high. Such scores identify any aspects of your lifestyle which would benefit from change.

AMBER ZONE

As with traffic lights, amber means proceed with caution. Consider ways in which you might reduce the risk by adopting appropriate procedures from our Long Life Heart programme. Above average scores for any of the 10 specific risk factors indicate areas which need the most immediate attention.

RED ZONE
This indicates the need for change and should give you cause for sensible concern rather than alarm. Begin working on our programme as soon as possible, concentrating on those risk factors where your scores were highest. Monitor progress every two or three months by repeating the risk assessment.

Why Those Questions Were Asked

Let's consider the statements and questions in greater detail to see why we included them in the assessment and what different scores indicate.

RISK FACTOR NO. 1 – WEIGHT
Statements 1–3
Even moderate obesity can lead to such serious health problems as high blood pressure and levels of cholesterol which damage the heart.

A useful measure of obesity is the Girth Test (Statement 1). Studies have shown that excess fat around the stomach, producing the unsightly paunch, carries a greater risk of heart disease than having fat thighs.

The risk of heart attack also increases significantly for men whose waist is larger than their hips and for women when their waist-to-hips ratio is greater than 4:5 (0.8) (statement 2).

We suggested that you *calculated* your ideal weight, instead

Assessing Your Risk Factors

of providing a standard height–weight chart, because the result is far more accurate for those of average build.

If you are of above average height or body build a more accurate result can be obtained by calculating your Body Mass Index or BMI. Unless mental arithmetic is your strong point a calculator will be helpful. Here's how to do it.

- Multiply your weight in pounds by 703.
- Divide the result by your height in inches.
- Divide by height for a second time. The result is your BMI.

Example
Height = 68 inches; Weight = 165 lbs.
BMI calculation is: 165 x 703 = 115,995.
 First division by 68 (height): 115,995/68 = 1705.8.
 Second division by 68: 1705.8/68 = BMI 25.1.

A BMI between 20 and 25 is normal. Should you wish to check it against your answer to Statement 3, score 0 if in the normal range; score 1 for a BMI between 26 and 28; 2 for a BMI of 29–30 and 3 for a BMI over 30. This result, obtained by some 34 million Americans, is a sign of 'medically significant obesity'.

Scores	Risk level
0–2	GREEN
3–5	AMBER
6–9	RED

RISK FACTOR NO. 2 – MOUTH SIGNS
Statements 4–12

These are only significant, so far as any increased risk of heart disease is concerned, following a heart attack. When present prior to an attack, they indicate a generally tense and nervous disposition, but not necessarily any increased risk of heart disease. Following an attack, however, they may occur as the result of stress and anxiety provoked by health fears and indicate damagingly high levels of physical arousal. We shall be discussing the link between coronary heart disease and such arousal in Chapter 4.

What your mouth reveals

The mouth is one of our most active bodily areas. We use it not only to eat, drink and speak but also to show our emotions. We express joy, astonishment, anger, doubt, disgust, shame, worry, hatred, misery and many other feelings by changing the tension in our lip muscles. The mouth's importance can be judged by looking at the amount of brain power devoted to it.

The mouth's importance was first recognized by Freud, who believed the oral stage, which occurs between the first and second years of life, was crucial to healthy development. During this period the infant's main method of communicating with the world, and obtaining pleasure, is through the mouth which can be used for chewing, sucking, kissing, eating and biting. With maturity, great efforts are often made to conceal our emotions by forming the face muscles into an expressionless mask. Mental tension produces oral tension and tense muscles are contracted muscles. We are all familiar with the tight, defensive smile of the anxious person or the deeply furrowed brow of the perplexed.

Signs in the tongue

The tongue is one of the most important speech muscles. It is shaped like an upturned boot, with the ankle part being attached to the floor of the mouth on which it rests in the relaxed state. Chronic tension, however, makes it stick to

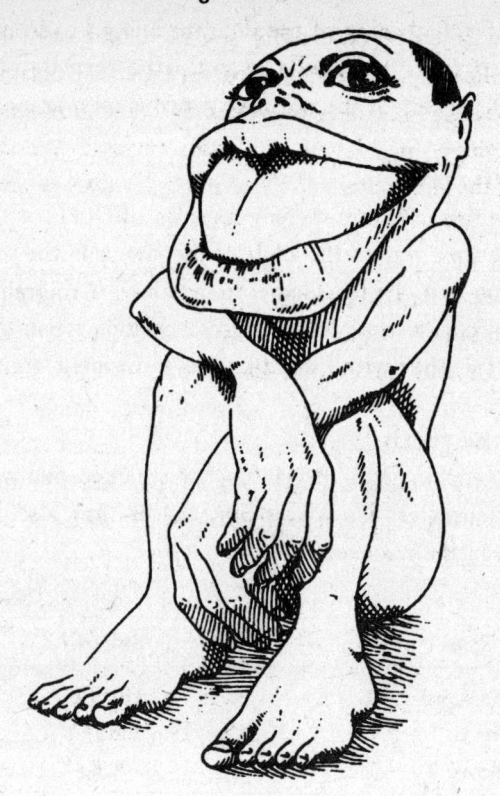

Figure 8 *If the size of our body parts reflected the amount of brain power devoted to them this is how we would look! Notice the disproportionate size of lips and tongue.*

the roof of the mouth resulting in a 'pie crust' appearance caused by continual pressure of the inner surface of the molar teeth which leave their imprint on its surface.

Signs in the cheeks
Tension in the lips and cheeks can also produce a white line on the inner surface of the mucous membrane, level with the biting surfaces of the teeth. This condition, called *leukoplakia*,

is due to the thickening of the delicate lining in response to continual friction. The lining may also be torn by nervous chewing or sucking at the sensitive mucous membrane.

Signs in the jaw
Continual tension makes the jaw muscles stiff and sore, often leading to pain either at the angle of the jaw or in the temple. This can be sufficiently severe to produce a migraine-like headache. Tension can also produce a clicking when the jaw is moved, together with limitations on movement.

Signs in the teeth
Constant clenching and/or grinding causes excessive wear on the biting surfaces, known as *attrition*, It may also loosen your teeth in their sockets.

Scores	Risk level
No score	GREEN
Score 1	AMBER
Score 2	RED

Releasing oral tensions
The higher your score, the greater the tension in your mouth. This usually indicates stress in other areas of the body and we shall be providing a detailed practical programme for dealing with this problem later in the book.

But if you obtained a score on this part of the assessment, it is a good idea to practise relaxing the muscles in your jaw, lips and tongue. Although accomplished easily and quickly, its overall effect on your health can be significant. Here's what you do:

1 Clench your teeth and notice the tension at the angle of the jaw and in the temple. If you find this difficult to identify – where you have become used to tension in these muscles the increase will be less noticeable – touch these muscles and note how hard they feel. Clench hard . . . harder. Hold this tension for 5 seconds.
2 Now let your jaw relax and hang loose. Notice the difference between tension and relaxation in these muscles.
3 Next tense your lips by pressing them tightly together. Compress them hard . . . harder. Hold for 5 seconds.
4 Relax. Allow your lips to rest gently together and, once again, notice the difference between tension and relaxation in these muscles.
5 Finally, tense your tongue by pressing the tip against the roof of the mouth. Press hard . . . harder. Hold for 5 seconds.
6 Relax. Allow your tongue to rest loosely in the bottom of the mouth.

Now that you have become more aware of the difference between oral tension and relaxation, turn your attention to the mouth a few times each day. You will then become more conscious of occasions when the muscles tense up.

The tongue may be pressed against the hard palate instead of being relaxed in the floor of the mouth. Your lips may be pressed firmly together, as if keeping a tight rein on what you might say. Your teeth may be clamped tightly together instead of there being about five millimetres of space between them.

RISK FACTOR NO. 3 – BLOOD PRESSURE
Statement 13

The meaning of blood pressure
As already mentioned, when your blood pressure is taken,

two measures – systolic and diastolic – are obtained. Systolic pressure is the power of your heart's pumping action while contracting and diastolic is the resting pressure between pulses, during which the heart fills with blood.

How blood pressure is taken
Blood pressure is usually measured in millimetres of mercury (mmHg). The upper arm is wrapped in a cuff which is then inflated to shut off the blood flowing down the arm's main (brachial) artery. Taking the wrist (radial) pulse as a guide, the doctor inflates the cuff until blood flow down the artery is blocked.

She deflates the cuff slowly, listening through a stethoscope until a series of rhythmic sounds are heard and then disappear again. The appearance of sounds represents systolic pressure and the disappearance diastolic pressure.

As mentioned earlier, when and where readings are taken is important, since not only does blood pressure vary at different times of day, but it is significantly increased by stress, exercise and sexual activity. Even the anxiety of having your BP taken distorts the results. Instead of relying on a single reading, especially if you are taking your own BP (see below), take several at different times of the day before concluding you are hypertensive.

When your BP is taken by a doctor or nurse, ask for the actual figures. British doctors often take a conservative attitude towards blood pressure, setting a higher figure for diagnosing hypertension than American practitioners.

What is normal blood pressure?
The World Health Organization defines normal (normotension) blood pressure as below 140mmHg systolic and below

90mmHg diastolic. In Europe and America the average blood pressure is 120/80mmHg.

What are the symptoms of hypertension?
Although many believe high blood pressure is always associated with headaches, dizziness and lethargy, such symptoms are an unreliable indicator of hypertension. They are as likely to be present in people with normal BP as among those with hypertension. It is possible to be seriously hypertensive, with a *diastolic* pressure of more than 115mmHg, without having any symptoms.

What causes hypertension?
In the vast majority of cases no reason can be found and it is referred to as *primary* or *essential* hypertension. For approximately 5 per cent of patients, however, high blood pressure is secondary to an underlying problem, such as kidney disease.

Diet plays a role in essential hypertension. Some studies suggest, for instance, that having too much salt in your diet leads to an increase in blood pressure. Statement 15 was included in the assessment for this reason.

Other factors are obesity, chronic stress and drinking too much alcohol (i.e. 37 or more standard units a week for men, and 25 or more for women).

What are the risks?
It is important to treat hypertension which poses a significant threat to health. The Framingham study, in Massachusetts, one of the most thorough ever undertaken, suggests the incidence of coronary heart disease rises by 20 per cent per 10mmHg increase in systolic pressure. At 160mmHg there is twice the risk found at 110mmHg.

A diastolic pressure of 110mmHg during middle age creates a one-in-five probability of death within five years when untreated. Men with high systolic pressure are more likely to die from heart disease even when their diastolic pressure is below the danger level.

Severe hypertension may be present in heart failure, while coronary heart disease is associated with mild to moderate hypertension.

Blood pressure greater than 160/95mmHg gives a three-fold increase in the risk of coronary heart disease and gives a four- to seven-fold chance of heart failure.

Scores	Risk level
No score	GREEN
Score 3	AMBER
Greater than 3	RED

Hypertension shortens your life not only from heart failure and strokes, but by damaging the kidneys which depend on the correct blood pressure to function efficiently. A below average BP poses no risk to health unless you are suffering from some other medical condition, such as a haemorrhage or burns.

What to do about hypertension

Knowing whether you have high blood pressure and, if so, the extent of the hypertension, is an essential starting-point on the road back to health. By monitoring levels regularly, you can check the progress being made on the road back to a healthy heart.

Have your BP taken regularly. Self-monitoring devices can be purchased at most chemists. Some do not even require an arm cuff, but work by measuring pressure via the finger. Most of those for non-professional use incorporate a microphone in the cuff to eliminate the need for a stethoscope. They provide a direct read-out of both systolic and diastolic pressure, either via liquid crystal display or by means of a pointer moving around a dial.

If using a home monitoring device, bear these precautions in mind:

- Have the meter's accuracy checked at least once a year. Studies suggest some types become inaccurate after regular use.
- Cuff size is important. Using too small a cuff can lead to an artificially high pressure being recorded.
- If you are overweight, a falsely high reading may be recorded. If thin, a falsely low one.
- Never take a reading immediately after brisk exercise – even climbing the stairs to your bedroom – eating a large meal, smoking, drinking tea or coffee, or having a bath.

Adopting the procedures described in our healthy heart programme should bring about a significant and lasting reduction in high blood pressure.

RISK FACTOR NO. 4 – CHOLESTEROL
Statement 14
With the publication, in 1984, of a 10-year, $150 million study by the US National Heart, Lung and Blood Institute in Washington, DC, any remaining doubts about a link between high blood cholesterol level and heart disease were removed. In countries with a low incidence of coronary heart disease, such as Japan, the mean level is below 5.2 mmol/l (200mg/100ml), which can be considered ideal.

Exactly what cholesterol is and what part it plays in heart disease will be described in later chapters.

Scores	Risk level
No score	GREEN
Score 3	AMBER
Greater than 3	RED

RISK FACTOR NO. 5 – DIET
Statements 15–19

A distinction needs to be made between the refined carbohydrates, particularly white sugar, present in most processed and manufactured foods, and unrefined carbohydrates found in brown rice, fresh fruit, vegetables, pasta and wholemeal bread. The former increase the risk of CHD while the latter are either neutral or enhance heart health.

The significance of drinking hard or soft water arises from a finding by the British Regional Heart Study, which has been monitoring several thousand men since 1978, of a link between tap water and heart disease.

After allowing for differences in climate and socioeconomic factors, researchers found a 10–15 per cent excess in cardiovascular deaths in very soft water areas. However, no differences were found in 13 towns which had artificially softened water and no physiological explanation for the apparent relationship has been suggested. It can, therefore, be seen as a very slight risk factor.

The importance of all aspects of diet in enhancing heart health will be discussed in Chapters 10 and 11.

Scores	Risk Level
0–4	GREEN
5–10	AMBER
11–16	RED

If your score on this section was more than 5, be sure to incorporate the suggestions we make into your regular eating pattern.

RISK FACTOR NO. 6 – THE FAMILY FACTOR
Statement 20

A long-term study of nearly 8,000 British males, by Professor Gerald Shaper of the Royal Free School of Medicine in London, showed a family influence in heart disease. Middle-aged men whose fathers died from this cause are twice as likely to have a heart attack.

If both parents died of a heart attack this risk increases by four-and-a-half times. This suggests that a genetic factor may be involved in some forms of heart disease, but the link is by no means established and other connected factors could be involved. Men whose parents had heart trouble are, for instance, more likely to smoke, have high blood cholesterol and hypertension.

In families where there is no incidence of heart disease some form of genetic protection is operating, which allows the overall assessment score to be reduced by 10 points. However, this should not be taken as an excuse to increase other risk factors.

Scores	Risk level
No score/points subtracted	GREEN
Score 2	AMBER
Score 5 and above	RED

RISK FACTOR NO. 7 – SMOKING
Statement 21
A lighted cigarette produces around 4,000 substances. Although attention is usually focused on just two of them, nicotine and carbon monoxide, many of the remaining chemicals are equally harmful. Some may be responsible for the furring up (atheroma) of the coronary arteries, which produces the high rate of heart disease among smokers.

Research shows that carbon monoxide promotes the build-up of the fatty plaque which leads to thrombosis. Men who smoke are slightly more at risk than women smokers and run about twice the risk of non-smokers. While it is a difficult habit to break, you must do so in order to safeguard your heart.

Scores	Risk Level
5 deducted from total	GREEN
5 added to total	AMBER
10–15 added to total	RED

RISK FACTOR NO. 8 – EXERCISE
Statement 22
The benefits of regular aerobic exercise in safeguarding the heart from disease are well-known. Following an attack you must, of course, proceed with care. Even so, the only way back to health is by gradually increasing the amount of exer-

cise taken. We shall be looking at this topic in detail in Chapter 12.

Scores	Risk level
5–3 deducted from total	GREEN
1 deducted from total	AMBER
3 added to total	RED

RISK FACTOR NO. 9 – PERSONALITY
Statements 23–33

These questions explored the extent to which you possess what psychologists call a Type A personality. Typical Type As are striving, ambitious, competitive, impatient, always pressed for time and try to do a great many things at once. Type A people seem to be more prone to heart disease than their behavioural opposites – the so-called Type Bs, who adopt a more easy-going, relaxed approach to life. Some studies suggest Type As have double the risk. As we shall explain, however, there is increasing evidence that what matters is not Type A behaviour as such, but aspects of personality found in some, but not all, the people who come into this category.

Scores	Risk level
0–15	GREEN
16–30	AMBER
31–50	RED

RISK FACTOR NO. 10 – ANGER
Statements 34–45

The role of anger, hostility and what we have termed the 'Type H' personality is fully discussed in the next chapter.

We believe these form a sub-group of Type As and that these people have the greatest risk of all.

Scores	Risk level
0–5	GREEN
6–19	AMBER
20–36	RED

If you scored 6 or more on this part of the assessment, it could be that your way of dealing with powerful negative emotions – especially anger – poses a significant risk to your health.

What you can do to reduce or eliminate this risk will be explained in Chapter 4.

4

PERSONALITY AND HEART DISEASE

Years before a cardiologist diagnosed Martin's heart disease, a psychologist might have made a very different but closely related diagnosis. The lifestyle of this ambitious, aggressive, 42-year-old company director – whose story we told in Chapter 1 – would have clearly labelled him a Type A personality. If your own score on statements 23–33 of our assessment was 16 or more, it's probable that you too are Type A.

What Is Type A Behaviour?

Behaviour we would today describe as typical Type A was noted by the Anglo-Canadian physician Sir William Osler in 1892. He described the typical coronary patient as 'keen and ambitious . . . [a man] whose engines are always set at full speed'.

Osler believed doctors might safely diagnose angina pectoris simply by observing the way a patient behaved as he walked into the consulting room!

During the 1940s Dr H. F. Dunbar, who coined the term *psychosomatic illness*, suggested the competitive, goal-directed, striving behaviour of heart disease patients was sufficiently consistent to constitute a 'coronary' personality.

These early studies were largely ignored by cardiologists, primarily because they were considered unscientific. Certainly the research methods were often highly dubious. In arriving at her far-reaching conclusions about the coronary personality, for example, Dr Dunbar relied on interviews with only 22 patients, half of them Jewish, and so the sample was not representative of the population as a whole.

Even when the studies were more rigorous, a major objection remained — all were retrospective. That is, the patients' personalities were only assessed *after* they had suffered a heart attack. Since this is obviously a highly stressful experience, it was hardly surprising that tests showed them to be suffering greater stress than non-sufferers. As Professor Ethel Roskies points out:

> *This after-the-fact diagnosis weakened the scientific validity of the finding, raising the possibility that the coronary personality was the result rather than the cause of heart disease.*

The situation changed in 1974 with the work of two American cardiologists at the Harold Brunn Institute of Mount Zion Hospital in San Francisco, Meyer Friedman and Ray Rosenman.

According to one story, their interest was aroused after an upholsterer, called to repair the chairs in their waiting room, commented that only the front few inches of each chair was worn. He asked what it was about their patients which caused them to perch right on the edge of their seats!

At the time this comment did not make much of an impression on them. But it came to mind a little later when they were investigating the role of dietary cholesterol and animal fat in heart disease, by studying the eating habits of married couples in the San Francisco Junior League. To their surprise although they found no differences in the dietary intake of cholesterol and animal fat between husbands and wives, the men suffered a far higher rate of coronary heart disease. One of the wives was not in the least surprised by these findings, however. She bluntly told the researchers that her husband's health problems could be explained in one word – stress.

At this point, so the story goes, Friedman and Rosenman recalled their waiting room chairs, worn down at the front by the agitated movements of their stressed patients, and the concept of Type A behaviour was born.

In their report they proposed that those at greatest risk of heart disease were characterized by 'an action–emotion complex that can be observed in any person who is aggressively involved in a chronic, incessant struggle to achieve more and more in less and less time, and if required to do so, against the opposing efforts of other things or persons'.

Their descriptions were remarkably similar to those of the nineteenth-century physician William Osler who commented:

> *A man who has early risen and late taken rest, who has eaten the bread of carefulness, striving for success in commercial, professional or political life . . . to him . . . the avenger comes through his arteries.*

Friedman and Rosenman also identified the Type B personality whose outlook, lifestyle and behaviour was the complete opposite – as shown on page 58.

Type A	Type B
• Restless	• Tranquil
• Hurrying	• Unhurried
• Impatient	• Patient
• Challenging	• Accepting
• Driven	• Content
• Tense	• Relaxed
• Competitive	• Non-competitive

The concept of Type A behaviour captured the imagination of many researchers and produced a host of studies, the majority supporting Friedman and Rosenman's conclusions. One, which included both men and women, white as well as blue-collar workers, showed that, over an eight-year period, male Type As aged between 45 and 64 were twice as likely to develop coronary heart disease as Type B men. This link was even stronger in women, where Type As stood three times the risk of coronary heart disease of their Type B counterparts.

In another US study, 35 out of 50 individuals with coronary heart disease were judged to be Type As. Comparable distributions were found by Soviet researchers where 82 per cent of heart patients were Type A.

COMING TO TERMS WITH TYPE A
By choosing the neutral labels Type A and Type B, some researchers believe Friedman and Rosenman hoped to avoid antagonizing psychiatrists and psychologists who might otherwise feel affronted at cardiologists trespassing into their professional domain by commenting on a 'psychological' phenomenon.

Were that their intention, it seems to have done little to defuse the controversy their proposals aroused, both in the medical community and among lay people. Professor Roskies suggests that one of the reasons for the vitriolic nature of the debate at times is that while we can easily accept that smoking, not taking enough exercise and eating the wrong kinds of food are unhealthy, almost everything about Type A behaviour seems praiseworthy. For people raised in the competitive culture of the West, a desire for success and achievement are considered positive and commendable.

'Can we really believe it is harmful to be energetic, ambitious. hardworking, and achievement-oriented?' asks Ethel Roskies. 'For many of us, these are virtues learned at our mothers' knees!'

The fact you are reading this book makes it likely you have many Type A characteristics and that your responses to the heart assessment placed you in the amber, perhaps even the red sections of the score chart.

If so, you may feel: 'This doesn't apply to me. I always know when and how to unwind. I only very occasionally place myself under too much pressure. I know when to say no.'

You may also protest that life will only be worthwhile so long as your Type A behaviour continues. This was certainly Martin's first reaction when confronted by the threat which his lifestyle posed. 'If I can't live the way I want,' he said angrily, 'what's the point of living at all?'

But the choice is not between a fast, stimulating and fulfilling lifestyle or settling for an uneventful, unexciting and unrewarding existence. You can enjoy life to the full without paying the price of, at best, your good health and at worst life itself. How this may be done will be described in the following chapters.

Furthermore, there is evidence that by no means *all* Type A individuals are placing themselves at the same level of risk.

Many high achievers, from all walks of life, have enjoyed a ripe old age. Industrialist Henry Ford, for example, lived to 84; and newspaper tycoon William Randolph Hearst to 88. Aviation engineer and industrialist Thomas Sopwith, designer of the Hurricane fighter and Lancaster bomber, survived to over 100. Among statesmen, both Germany's Konrad Adenauer and Winston Churchill lived to 91.

In our view what matters more than being competitive is the way in which negative emotions, such as distrust, suspicion, cynicism, anger and frustration are handled. There appears to be a sub-group within the Type A personality for whom both the risk of coronary heart disease is greater and, following an attack, the prospect of a successful recovery less likely. As we explained in the previous chapter, we have decided to call these high CHD risk achievers the Type H. H stands here for Hostility, for Hurrying and for Humourlessness — the three key characteristics which distinguish the unhealthy from the healthy Type A.

A score of 6 or more on statements 34–45 suggests you too are a Type H. If so, there's good reason to stop and take stock of your life, but no cause for undue worry.

By making certain changes in outlook and lifestyle you can reduce the risk of heart disease or help ensure a good recovery following an attack.

The Type H Personality

In 1960 a major study was begun to test the capacity of Type A behaviour patterns to predict heart disease. Known as the Western Collaborative Group Study (WCGS) it followed 3,154 apparently healthy Californian males, aged from 39 to

59, who were mainly white, middle- and upper-class executives. On entry to the study 1,589 of them were classified as Type As, the remainder as calmer, easy-going, less competitive Type Bs. Some nine years later, 257 of the Type As had developed coronary heart disease compared with only 79 Type Bs. In other words As had more than double the risk of developing heart disease. Furthermore, the death rate among Type A coronary heart disease patients was also higher. Of the 25 deaths due to heart disease which occurred during the study, 22 were among Type As. Careful analysis of the data showed that these differences could not be blamed on other risk factors, such as smoking or diet.

But this is not the full story. While the incidence of coronary heart disease among Type As was more than double, it was also true that the hearts of 89 per cent of those initially considered at high risk remained healthy. In 1977 a group of researchers looked at a smaller group of men from the original WCGS study, all of whom had suffered a heart attack over a four-year period, and compared them with a sample of healthy males. They found them to have answered significantly differently on seven of the original questions designed to identify Type A behaviour. All were related to anger or hostility. A reanalysis of the original data confirmed this finding. The factor of greatest importance was not whether a person always seemed pressed for time, ate their meals rapidly, was energetic or a workaholic, but their 'potential for hostility'. What does this imply?

One of the most notoriously hostile individuals of recent years has been the rabble rousing anti-Communist Senator Joseph McCarthy who died of a heart attack in 1957 at the young age of 48. After McCarthy's death, friends blamed his early demise on enemies who had broken his health and crushed his spirit.

Medical research suggests, however, that the Senator from Wisconsin was struck down not by some vindictive enemy but his own angry, cynical and suspicious nature. He was his own most deadly foe, *New York Times* writer William S. White described him as 'an engine of outward fury operating in an inner mode'.

In a study at Duke University Medical Centre, in Durham, North Carolina, psychiatrists analysed responses to a standard personality test completed, some 20 years earlier, by 500 middle-aged and older people. Among the traits analysed was one related to suspicion. They found that, after controlling for risks such as smoking, exercise and high cholesterol levels, those subjects who scored high on this factor were 40 per cent more likely to die of heart disease within the next 15 years than the low scorers. People with high scores tend to be aggressive, critical, dogmatic, irritable and rigid in their thinking. They hold grudges, do not easily forgive or forget, worry about what people say behind their backs and take criticism badly. Low scorers, by comparison, are tolerant, accepting and adaptable. 'McCarthy's way of projecting suspicions onto other people illustrates a high hostility factor,' comments Dr William Lohss, a psychologist at the Institute for Personality and Ability Testing in Champaign, Illinois.

Psychologist John Barefoot believes such people often create a self-fulfilling prophecy by antagonizing those around them. This leaves them with few friends and little social support, two factors known to increase the chances of stress-related illness in general, and coronary heart disease in particular.

COMING TO TERMS WITH BEING TYPE H
Even if your responses to hostility statements produced a score in the amber or red zones this does not mean you share

the Senator's unattractive personality. As with Type A behaviour, Type H behaviour lies on a continuum. At one end of it are friendly, trusting individuals while at the opposite pole are located the excessively cynical, extremely hostile, furiously angry and deeply mistrustful. Unless you obtained a maximum (36) or minimum (0) score on statements 34–45, you too will be somewhere between these poles.

As mentioned above, there are three major aspects to the Type H personality – Hostility, Hurrying and lack of Humour.

Hostility

This can reveal itself as anger, cynicism, distrust, guilt, suspicion and aggression. There will, of course, always be circumstances in which one is justified in being cynical, where it is safer to be distrustful, reasonable to feel guilty and right to become angry. Hostility only poses a threat to the heart when it is a *habitual* reaction to life instead of an occasional response to some unusual situation.

You may recall from Chapter 1, that Martin's heart attack occurred when he was having a blazing row with his driver over the late arrival of a company car. But such conflicts were far from uncommon. He took a pride in being a tough, aggressive individual whom it was unwise to cross or anger.

Interestingly, the famous eighteenth-century surgeon John Hunter, a blunt, impatient individual, suffered from angina pectoris for more than 20 years. But he only succumbed to a heart attack while engaged in a furious row over students' fees.

As damaging as openly expressed rage is inwardly directed anger, which may take the form of guilt, self-loathing, disgust or shame. All are emotions reflecting hostility towards oneself for having said or done, or failed to say or do, something important.

During the early 1970s, Dr Mary Julius and her colleagues from the University of Michigan surveyed some 700 men and women living in the small town of Tecumseh, Michigan. Twelve years later they rechecked them and found people with high blood pressure who suppressed their anger during family fights were twice as likely to have died during the intervening period. This was true for all age groups and both sexes, irrespective of other risk factors. 'It's the combination of marital stress, suppressed anger and high blood pressure that appears to place people at the greatest risk,' comments Dr Julius.

In any anger-arousing situation, one has the choice of suppressing angry feelings by turning them inward, venting one's anger or dealing with the feelings adaptively without allowing yourself to experience the artery-damaging arousal which anger brings. The third way is the *only* response that can safeguard your heart.

We emphasize this because so many people believe that outwardly expressed anger is, somehow, healthier and less harmful than repressed, inwardly directed, fury. This is simply not the case. Whether the anger is allowed to smoulder, unnoticed by any but yourself, or expresses itself in furious outbursts of rage the damage done to the cardiovascular system remains the same.

The strategy by which you can be healthily assertive without becoming harmfully hostile and angry is termed 'reflective coping' and it is the only way of safeguarding your heart. 'The key issue is not the amount or degree of anger, but how you cope,' says Duke University researcher Dr Ernest Harburg.

Let us repeat the crucial message:

> THE ONLY WAY TO SAVE YOUR HEART AND YOUR LIFE IS NOT TO FEEL ANGER AT ALL. ANGER OUT IS AS DANGEROUS AS ANGER IN.

This does not mean turning into a doormat and allowing everybody to walk all over you. Nor does it mean you can never feel strongly, deeply, passionately about issues of concern. But all these positive feelings can be experienced and expressed without any resort to hostility. How this may be done will be explained in Chapter 7.

Hurrying

A characteristic found in both the Type A and the Type H is a great sense of time pressure. The difference is that anything which frustrates the Type H in their onward rush through life tends to produce high levels of anger, directed at themselves or others. Type Hs will set themselves impossible deadlines and unworkable schedules. They will cheerfully accept two tough work assignments which demand they be in different places at virtually the same time.

Like the White Rabbit in *Alice in Wonderland* they are gasping: 'I'm late . . . I'm late' as they race helter skelter from one demanding task to the next. They drive quickly, get furious when kept waiting in a queue, become wild with pent-up frustrations and worry if stuck in a traffic jam.

They'll always leave for appointments at the very last minute, jumping onto trains as they pull away from the station, being the last to arrive at airports, appointments, theatres and restaurants. They'll usually try to do two or more things at the same time, reading notes when speaking on the phone, completing reports as they grab a sandwich, talking on radio phones when driving in rush-hour traffic.

Their speech is characterized by a machine-gun rapid delivery, often delivered as they stride briskly between appointments, hastening themselves with ever increasing speed toward ill health and an early grave.

Humourlessness

By this we do not mean an inability to enjoy oneself or laugh at a good joke. What is implied is more the inability to laugh at oneself, to see the funny, absurd or ridiculous side of even serious endeavours.

It may be that 'taking oneself seriously' is essential for entrepreneurial success. If you want to make a fortune manufacturing widgets, it's essential to regard widgets as the only things in life of real importance.

TYPE H AND THE UNHEALTHY HEART

But how can such feelings damage our physical health? How can powerful, yet seemingly intangible emotions bring about anything as obviously real and potentially fatal as coronary heart disease?

The link is a hormone called noradrenaline and the theory which describes its potentially fatal influence on the heart is termed the *noradrenaline hypothesis*.

In the next chapter we shall explain exactly what this is, how it affects you and why learning to control negative emotions in a positive manner is the first, essential, step to a healthy heart.

5

HEART AND MIND

When William Harvey, seventeenth-century discoverer of the circulation of the blood, wrote: 'Every affection of the mind that is attended with either pain or pleasure, hope or fear, is the cause of an agitation whose influence extends to the heart', he was echoing the romantic belief that passion has its focus in the human heart. This may burst with love, be warmed by kindness, chilled by despair and broken by grief. For centuries doctors have agreed with romantic novelists that one really can die of a 'broken' heart. A day after the death of actress Beatrice Lilly, at the age of 94, for example, her devoted friend and companion for 40 years also died. A friend of 66-year-old ex-marine John Huck explained: 'He lost the will to live.'

Such cases are far from rare. Widows and widowers often follow their dead spouse rapidly to the grave. One study showed the death rates of bereaved partners was 12 times higher than among the non-bereaved. During the 1970s the risk of heart disease was found to be two or three times higher in men suffering depression, anxiety or nervousness.

In a more recent study 2,300 male heart disease patients were given detailed interviews and followed over a three-year period. Interview questions probed for such stressors as loneliness, unhappiness at work, recent retirement, poor marriage, divorce, money worries and actual physical assaults, for instance a mugging. The probability of death in patients with a highly stressful life and few friends was *six times* greater than for those with many friends and less stress.

We have become so used to regarding illness as something produced by the invasion of a virus or bacteria that it can be difficult to accept we are no less capable of inflicting as much – indeed often far more – harm on ourselves. Harder still when positive virtues, such as hard work, or human qualities like anger, are concerned.

Hostility and Heart Disease

The links forming a chain between feelings and coronary heart disease are easily remembered because all begin with A. They are: arousal, anger, adrenaline, angina, arrhythmia, atheroma.

AROUSAL
If we imagine a continuum with deep sleep at one end, moving through drowsiness to feeling awake and alert, then progressing to edginess, tension, irritability, anxiety, fear, anger and finally panic or rage, we can see there are different levels of arousal.

Whether or not we suffer from heart disease and other stress-related illness depends on the frequency, duration and intensity of this arousal.

Fighting and fleeing
When danger threatens, the body undergoes important physical changes. Our heart beats faster, we breathe more

rapidly, sweating increases, blood drains away from small blood vessels directly beneath the skin (which is why we grow pale with fright) and is directed to the muscles. Digestion slows down, making our mouth go dry and producing those familiar butterflies in the stomach.

When triggered by a situation which is not objectively dangerous – such as in a phobia – or where neither fighting nor fleeing are possible, for instance when criticized by an angry superior, these bodily changes are both distressing and unhelpful. In a truly hazardous situation, however, they can prove a life-saver. The muscles have greater strength and stamina, the brain is more alert, reaction times are shorter, perception more acute, courage greater, endurance improved. Under such circumstances the human body becomes capable of feats which, in the non-aroused state, might prove impossible.

A pair of torn shorts

Although tattered and minus their seat, zoologist Dr Murray Watson cherishes these old bush shorts as a souvenir of his death-defying leap. While studying elephants in Kenya's Tsavo National Park, 26-year-old Murray Watson's Land-Rover broke down on his way back to camp one evening. Left with the choice of spending a chilly night in the truck or covering the last mile home on foot he decided to walk. A few hundred yards later he was bitterly regretting his decision.

Stumbling along a dirt track in semi-darkness, he heard the padding feet and grunting breaths of a hyena pack close on his heels. Murray Watson started running, knowing there was no way he could outrace them. As they closed for the kill, the young zoologist suddenly saw the branch of a tree several yards off the ground. With a flying leap he managed to grasp it and haul himself to safety. As he did so the pack leader's teeth closed around the seat of his pants and tore it away. Murray Watson spent an uncomfortable night clinging to the branch, while the hyenas circled below. At dawn, when they disappeared into the bush, he made his remarkable discovery. The branch which had saved his life was a good 12 feet above the ground. Having scrambled down there was no way in which he could get back up again. Jump as high as he might, his outstretched fingers remained well below the branch. Today his bush shorts provide a powerful reminder of his narrow brush with death and the potential of the human body when aroused by the fight or flight mechanism.

Fight or flight

Walter Cannon, a Harvard Medical School physiologist who made a special study of the fight and flight response, named the hormone responsible for it *adrenin* and showed it was found in two small adrenal glands, shaped like flattened triangles, located above each kidney. We now know that what Cannon called adrenin is actually two substances – *noradrenaline* and *adrenaline** – collectively known as *catecholamines*. While the adrenal glands mainly produce adrenaline, noradrenaline is primarily released by the ends of certain nerve fibres called *post-ganglionic sympathetic nerves*.

This requires some further explanation. The nervous system, as most people know, is the means by which messages from the brain are transmitted to all parts of the body. They serve a similar purpose to telephone lines conveying orders from head office to various departments in a factory as well as messages back to the brain from these departments.

---

* In America they are known as *norepinephrine* and *epinephrine*.

There are two main divisions. One, our *voluntary nervous system*, is used for sending commands from brain to muscles. While the voluntary nerves are involved in communicating conscious orders – such as the instructions to turn the pages in this book – the other division, called the *autonomic nervous system* (ANS), is concerned with regulating such essential but involuntary functions as heart beat, breathing and digestion. The ANS can be likened to an aircraft's automatic pilot in that it takes care of the routine tasks needed to 'fly' our body, so liberating the 'thinking' brain for more intellectually demanding tasks. Just consider for a moment how impossible life would be if one had consciously to instruct the heart to beat once each second or command the lungs to fill with air 17 times a minute!

The ANS operates, for the most part, independently of conscious control. You cannot, for instance, order your heart to stop beating or your digestive system to stop digesting food.

A level of arousal appropriate to the demands of our surroundings can be maintained thanks to a balancing act between two branches of the ANS. One, the *parasympathetic*, slows things down and another, the *sympathetic* branch, speeds things up. Together they produce a steady state known as *homoeostasis*.

The two branches of the ANS can be likened to the reins on a horse. If a rider applies equal pressure to each rein the animal continues in a straight line. But a sharp tug on either rein will cause it to veer sharply to left or right.

Another way of looking at it is as the two sides of a balance.

ADRENALINE AND NORADRENALINE

Although these hormones have similar structures, their effects are different. When we feel anxious, adrenaline

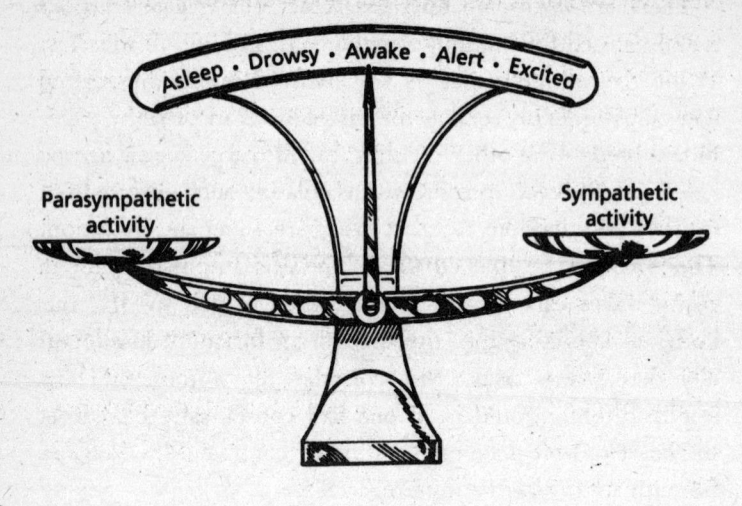

Figure 9 The arousal–relaxation balance.

prepares us for flight. When we feel angry, noradrenaline primes the body for fight.

In most threatening situations it would be an oversimplification to say there is any such thing as a pure emotion of either rage or fear. We typically alternate between anxiety and anger. In some cases there may also be a measure of depression as well.

These mixed emotions create a mixture of catecholamines, including both adrenaline and noradrenaline. When depression is present an additional hormone, cortisol, is added to the biochemical cocktail. Here, however, we shall focus on the fight or flight hormones, noradrenaline and adrenaline.

Anger and noradrenaline

Unlike adrenaline, which makes us feel tense and edgy, the subjective effects of noradrenaline are much less distressing in many ways, exhilarating and exciting. Because of this it is often referred to as the 'kick' hormone, an effect which gives it addictive qualities. People can quickly become dependent on noradrenaline in order to feel alert, alive and performing well. Noradrenaline revives drooping spirits, combats fatigue and allows us to perform for longer.

But, as with any addiction, there is a price to pay. Those who become hooked can never relax because their systems are perpetually hyperaroused: the condition found in Type A behaviour.

Noradrenaline is not only physically rewarding. In a society which so powerfully encourages high achievers to produce more and more in less and less time, being a noradrenaline junkie also leads to fame and fortune. But here, too, there is a high price to pay.

Deadlines and work pressure generate feelings of anger and frustration whenever obstacles arise to threaten these goals. As the physical system becomes fatigued, those hooked on noradrenaline use artificial aids to boost its output and so revive flagging energy levels. The nicotine in cigarettes causes the body to release more noradrenaline – which explains the popularity of brands high in nicotine among Type As.

Caffeine in coffee and tea are stimulating for the same reason: they promote noradrenaline. Taking part or viewing exciting sports has the same effect, so too does watching violent films or TV programmes. Working to a demanding schedule, driving at speed and racing to keep appointments all provide a similar boost.

Anger, as the Bible warns us, is the deadliest of sins. In a society where few of us can ever vent that rage, it is also the most lethal.

One of the present authors (John Storey) began to be interested in the effects of noradrenaline when he was carrying out research into stress among dentists. During the study he collected blood from dental surgeons at the start and end of their working day. When the blood was spun at high speed to separate the cells from the plasma, the difference between the two samples was striking. In blood drawn before the day began, the plasma was clear. In that taken eight hours later it was milky grey, a cloudiness caused by suspended particles of fat. Similar results were also obtained from the blood of racing drivers. Prior to the start of a race it was clear, afterwards cloudy.

To exert their effect catecholamines must combine with receptors on the cells with which they act. Some substances have a molecular structure very similar to catecholamines, which allows them to lock onto the receptors in the same way that the correctly shaped key will fit into and turn a lock. These substances are called beta receptor blockers. Just as you can only insert one key at a time into a lock, once they have occupied a receptor there is no room for the catecholamines. Although these continue to be produced, their effect is neutralized.

When Drs Malcolm Carruthers and Peter Taggert administered small doses of the beta-blocker oxprenolol to professional racing drivers one hour before the start of a race, they found that not only was the rapid pulse rate suppressed – the expected effect of taking a beta blocker – but that their blood plasma was as clear and free from fatty acids after the race as it had been beforehand.

In a further study they monitored arousal in public speakers, finding a rapid heart rate, abnormalities in rhythm and increases in both plasma catecholamines and free fatty acids. Most interesting was that prior to speaking total catecholamines levels were raised, the chief increase being in adrenaline.

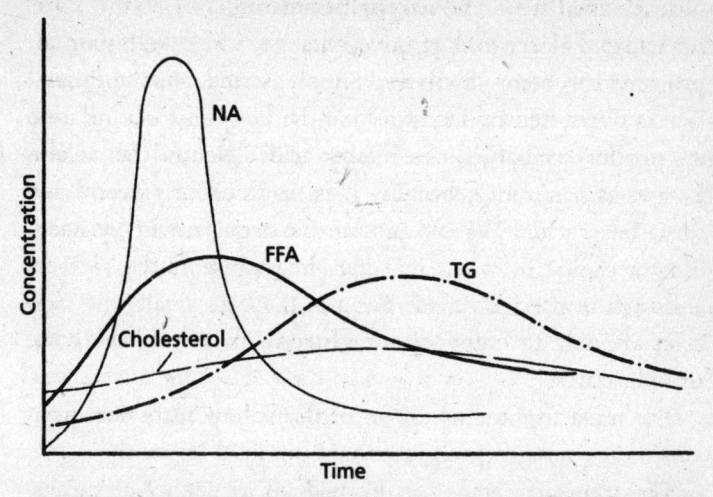

Figure 10 *Chart illustrating how the concentration of free fatty acids (FFA) in the blood plasma rises as a response to a sudden surge of noradrenaline (NA). Triglyceride (TG) concentrations are also affected.*

After they had finished, however, adrenaline remained the same while noradrenaline levels rose significantly. It appears that, prior to speaking, anxiety was the major emotion but during the speech they experienced a more aggressive, competitive feeling. When these speakers were given beta-blockers their blood plasma remained clear of lipids – a further demonstration of the way in which noradrenaline breaks down neutral fat to produce harmful free fatty acids.

What do public speakers and racing drivers have in common?

The answer is a particular type of stress: the stress of hostility. This may express itself in the competitive spirit as an intense desire to win. It may find expression as frustration when ambitions are thwarted; anger towards those held responsible for preventing one's success or guilt and self-blame at having failed.

Noradrenaline – the anger hormone

Let's take a closer look at noradrenaline. It has the important property of being lipolytic. Simply stated, this means it breaks down neutral fat, stored in the body's fat depots, into its smaller constituent free fatty acids. Neutral fat is also known as *triglyceride*, because it is made up of glycerol and three fatty acids. We can picture the arrangement by imagining a capital E, where the upright represents the glycerol and each arm a fatty acid. Because they are small, the fatty acids are able to enter the bloodstream, which is where the trouble starts.

The most frightening aspect of this is how little noradrenaline is required to produce maximum lipid response.

The free fatty acids not burned up as energy are transported to the liver and converted into triglyceride (neutral fat). They are not stored in the liver, however, but recirculated back into the blood plasma as lipoproteins – lipid-bearing particles. These particles can be divided into two main types: high density lipoproteins (HDL) and low density lipoproteins (LDL).

High density lipoproteins

These transport fats *away* from the arterial wall, thereby protecting it from damage. Because of this HDLs are beneficial to health.

Low density lipoproteins

These carry lipids *into* the arterial wall, and are therefore damaging to the health. For adults a LDL level below 3.4 mmol/l (130mg/100ml) and HDL levels above 1.3 mmol/l (50mg/100ml) reduce the risk of heart disease. HDL levels are increased by exercise but reduced by smoking, obesity and taking the contraceptive pill.

Type A people have a high level of these fats in their blood, a fact which used to be blamed on poor diet. Yet racing drivers, who often fast before a race, may still have high levels in their blood because they are produced internally.

Blood clot hazards

Also present in the blood are cells called platelets which have a vital role to play in the clotting mechanism. During fight and flight the speed of clotting increases, in order to minimize blood loss should any injury occur. For our primitive ancestors this was of value and greatly increased their chances of survival. In modern man – usually unable to fight or flee when stressed – it poses a hazard to health and may provide yet another nail for the coffin created by coronary heart disease.

High levels of free fatty acids cause the platelets to stick together, encouraging blood to clot on the inside of the vessel as we simmer in silence. High levels of fatty acids also cause the heart to beat irregularly (*arrhythmia*).

ATHEROMA

The final link in the chain, this begins during childhood with fatty streaks on the lining of the artery.

These coalesce to form the plaques mentioned earlier, which can then become infiltrated by fibrous tissue to varying degrees: some plaques are mostly fibrous while others are mainly fatty. A haemorrhage into the plaque can cause a sudden increase in its size, obstructing blood flow and bringing about a heart attack.

Later in life a build-up of calcium (a process called *calcification*) may occur, making the arteries hard and inelastic.

In time a plaque can rupture into the lumen of the artery

to form an ulcer – the medical term for a defect on the surface of an organ or tissue. If this ulcer triggers defensive blood clotting, a thrombosis results, posing a further grave threat to health.

Atheroma is often found at points where vessels branch, blood flow is interrupted and turbulence occurs. The arteries most prone to the development of atheroma are those serving the heart, brain and legs.

In some cases other factors are at work. Strong emotions may cause the coronary artery to go into spasm, since noradrenaline has a powerful constricting action on blood vessels. In an already diseased artery this can prove the final straw. It also means that symptoms of angina may not always match the degree of blocking in a coronary artery. In fact one can have quite advanced coronary artery disease with no symptoms and a lot of symptoms with little atheroma.

An additional danger posed by powerful emotions, and one to which we will return in a later chapter, is the overbreathing which occurs when one is angry or afraid.

Rapid, shallow breathing removes carbon dioxide from the blood, causing it to become alkaline. This also triggers spasms of the blood vessels, not only in the heart but also the brain.

Finally, strong emotions can affect the electrical stability of the heart, resulting in the irregular beating known as an arrhythmia. A violent argument may end in sudden death without a blow being struck and with a relatively healthy heart being found at post mortem.

THE RISKS OF HEART DISEASE
As we have seen, a popular approach to the prevention of coronary heart disease is to look at the risk factors – smoking, high blood pressure, obesity and high blood lipids –

Heart and Mind

which we assessed in our questionnaire. However, all these factors are caused by the same thing – hyperarousal.

Hyperarousal raises the blood pressure and blood lipids. People smoke, drink and overeat as a means of lowering their arousal.

Just as we used the letter E to explain the structure of the triglyceride, so we can use it to point the way to health-giving patterns of behaviour. The keys to a healthy heart are emotions, eating, exercise. By this we mean:

- Controlling negative emotions
- Eating prudently
- Exercising moderately but regularly.

The remainder of this book is devoted to providing you with the knowledge and practical skills necessary for putting those three basic instructions into action.

6

CREATIVE STRESS MANAGEMENT

Centuries before the birth of Christ, Hippocrates, the Greek physician of Kos and father of medicine, developed the first scientific theory of disease. Previously illness had been seen as the result of possession by demons. But Hippocrates argued that ill health arose through an imbalance of four fluids, or humours: blood, black and yellow bile, and phlegm. An excess of black bile led to depression and melancholy; too much blood produced a sanguine disposition; excessive yellow bile resulted in a jaundiced view of the world, while surplus phlegm created a calm, phlegmatic character. We still reflect these ancient ideas when describing somebody as being 'out of humour'.

The Enemy Within

Although Hippocrates' ideas were wrong in detail, his concept was a good one. Later, however, attention was focused on the enemy without, as scientists began to discover the role played in disease by bacteria, viruses and other micro-organisms.

In the nineteenth century Claude Bernard, a French physiologist, redirected attention to the importance of a person's 'internal environment', that is the blood and other fluids which bathe our cells. Our very survival demands that this inner state be held constant even when our surroundings are constantly changing.

The body's core temperature, for example, must remain at 37°C (98.4°F) for the chemical reactions on which life depends to occur. A prolonged fall (hypothermia) or rise (fever) in temperature, even if by only a few degrees, leads to coma and death. So efficient is our body's thermostatic control mechanism that the internal temperature of a desert nomad and Arctic hunter are identical.

Other limiting ranges which the body is programmed to maintain include BP: the arteries cannot withstand a pressure above 400/200 or the system function below 60/30. Electrical power to the brain must not fluctuate greatly from 20 watts; carbon dioxide in the air we breathe must not exceed 6 per cent.

Walter Cannon, a Harvard physiologist, named this steady state *homoeostasis* and described our remarkable capacity for maintaining it as 'wisdom of the body'.

STRESS AND HOMOEOSTASIS

In the last chapter we explained that the sympathetic and parasympathetic branch of the ANS work together to maintain this steady state of homoeostasis.

Stress, therefore, is anything which, by disturbing this equilibrium, compels the system to draw on its energy reserves in order to maintain homoeostasis. If constantly challenged by a wide range of stressors we will eventually exhaust the body's ability to sustain the steady internal state.

We can liken what happens to an elastic band which is constantly stretched. After a while the band no longer returns to its original length and, if the stretching continues, eventually snaps.

Chronic stress resulting from daily challenges and harassments has a similar effect on our emotional, intellectual and physical resistance. Stress which is too frequent, too intense too long-lasting will eventually result in disease, damage and death.

The resetting of the homoeostatic mechanisms following prolonged stress can be compared to that overstretched elastic band.

When stressed, blood pressure, blood lipids and many other biochemical and physiological variables become elevated. Tragically our whole society is so chronically stressed that these unnaturally raised levels are now accepted as normal because they occur in the vast majority of people.

Doctors consider a blood cholesterol level of 6 mmol/litre as normal, despite the fact that a much safer figure would be 5 mmol/litre. Similarly, Western medicine accepts as normal a rise in systolic blood pressure of 1 millimetre of mercury per year. This means that at age 55 a systolic pressure of 155mm of mercury would not be regarded as abnormal. Yet in non-industrialized countries blood pressure actually falls with age. The only reason for the steady increase found in Western society is that by living in a perpetual state of hyper-arousal, we reset the homoeostatic mechanisms to an ever higher level.

The same applies to pulse rate, where between 70 and 80 beats per minute are held to be consistent with good health. If you are mentally and physically fit, however, most tasks can be performed effectively at levels ranging between 50 and 60.

Recall the three billion times our heart beats in the average life span and then calculate the extra years you could enjoy if your heart was allowed to beat 10 fewer times per minute, or 5,256,000 fewer beats per year!

CREATIVE STRESS MANAGEMENT

Stress can be friend or foe. When allowed to take control it will undermine your performance and harm your health. If managed correctly, however, stress can actually enhance mental physical functioning, helping you to enjoy a longer, healthier and happier life.

Each of us has a peak performance stress level (PPSL). This represents the level of arousal required to perform a particular task efficiently with no harmful physical or mental effects. The PPSL varies from one task to the next. In general the more intellectually demanding a challenge, the lower the optimum level of arousal. When working for any length of time at above, or below, our PPSL we become distressed, find it hard to cope or concentrate, feel control slipping from our grasp and perform less and less successfully.

As stress increases we become more and more anxious, confused, frustrated and unable to cope with the demands being made on our time and energy. Judgement is adversely affected and we start making ill-considered and sometimes disastrous decisions. The solutions found to personal or professional problems become inappropriate and unsatisfactory. Memory and concentration are impaired until even well-known facts and figures become harder to bring to mind, while recall itself is less accurate.

Understress, usually found in tedious, repetitive tasks, is as harmful to well-being as the stress overload which occurs when we attempt to deal with too many emotional and/or physical demands. When working for long periods below our PPSL, we feel bored, apathetic and lacking in motivation.

We may feel depressed, have little appetite and sleep poorly despite constant feelings of fatigue. The mind seems to work more sluggishly, making it hard to reach decisions or even bother to search for answers to problems. Even a minor difficulty or set-back can come to seem like an insurmountable obstacle.

Creative stress management involves maintaining your level of arousal at a point where you feel stimulated rather than threatened by life's challenges.

STRESS AND HELPLESSNESS
Perhaps the most disturbing aspects of working outside the PPSL is a feeling that control over events is slipping from our grasp. Such a sensation is always highly stressful. One reason why many people fear flying is that, for the duration of the flight, they have no control over what happens. Their destiny is in the hands of anonymous human beings on the flight deck.

When Columbia University sociologist Robert Karasek examined the health and work records of American and Swedish males, he found a clear link between cardiovascular disease and the work people did. In some cases this association was so significant certain occupations could virtually be labelled as high-risk-heart-attack jobs. They were not, however, careers normally regarded as posing such a risk. It was not only jet-setting executives or Type A entrepreneurs who proved in greatest danger but also assembly-line workers and telephone company service engineers.

'The myth is that managers are at highest risk,' says Dr Karasek. 'But really they aren't. This is because they have optimal control over their jobs.'

Assembly line workers and phone company men dealing with customer complaints, by comparison, are in the most stressful of situations, having responsibility without power. They are unable to develop their own working routine or adopt preferred ways of tackling jobs, nor do they have the means to reduce tension. Employees dealing with the public must often face criticism and abuse for problems which were not of their making and which they have little or no authority to put right.

STRESS AND BURN-OUT
The longer we are obliged to function above or below our PPSL, the greater the danger of experiencing burn-out stress syndrome or BOSS. Common symptoms of BOSS include:

- Exhaustion – loss of energy, debilitation, fatigue.
- Distrust and cynicism increase, making it harder to maintain close personal relationships. People suffering BOSS feel increasingly irritable, have difficulty coping with even minor frustrations and tend to focus on their failures rather than successes.
- Depression, poor morale and a sense of hopelessness are also common, and lead to a loss of confidence and low self-esteem.
- Health problems, including upset digestion; aching muscles, especially in the lower back and neck; headaches; and missed menstrual periods are often encountered. The heart is, of course, also put at risk.
- In an attempt to cope with BOSS, victims resort to smoking more cigarettes, consuming more alcohol and taking drugs, both medically prescribed and otherwise. Often they also eat more. This, combined with lack of energy and a reluctance to take exercise, leads to weight problems, so placing the heart under further strain.

As you will appreciate, BOSS quickly becomes a self-reinforcing process, with negative attitudes and actions leading to further discouragement and withdrawal.

CHRONIC STRESS AND ILL HEALTH

In all degenerative diseases there is what doctors term a long *prodromal* period during which the steady state has been disrupted but no organic disease is yet apparent. What normally happens is that the stressed person goes to the doctor complaining of feeling generally unwell.

This is the stage of non-specific illness. The doctor may prescribe a drug to quieten the mind (a tranquillizer) or the body (a beta-blocker). This symptomatic treatment does nothing to resolve the root cause of the condition and, after a brief period of improvement, the symptoms recur. The doctor may then suggest taking life easier or having a holiday, advice which is usually difficult – if not impossible – to follow.

If you are stressed at work, the cause of that stress is not going to disappear while you are away for a couple of weeks, and it is hard to relax while worrying that work is being neglected and important tasks left undone. Furthermore, the very reason why you are tense is because you do not know how to relax in the first place.

A point to remember is that it is not the work you do that makes you stressed but the effort invested in it. Many of us become overaroused for the task we are performing. We attempt to do too much in too short a period of time and then worry about meeting pressing deadlines.

In a study of senior British executives, sociologist Michael Young found them likely to be overstretched after 'committing themselves to an 8-day week or 30-hour day, always trying to do too much'. As a result they were constantly fighting the clock and experiencing the modern plague of 'hurry sickness'. In his book *The Metronomic Society*, he reports:

> *They were rushing from one event without time to savour anything or take a well-considered decision. They did not allow themselves think about the future of their companies, their colleagues or themselves; they were continually harassed, even though they were never supposed to look as though they were; and they had no holidays from the pressure of time . . . claiming to have no time was a means of asserting status, measured by panting.*

At the end of a day spent racing to get too many things done, we go to bed worrying whether we'll get enough sleep to keep going the next day. But although tired all day, getting into bed suddenly wakes us up again and sleep is the last thing on our mind. Instead we lie fretting over all the things which have gone wrong during the day or could go wrong in the day ahead.

When chronic stress drives us to the point of breakdown, signs and symptoms of disease occur. At this point the sufferer, having started to crack up, looks to the doctor to stick him or her back together again. Unfortunately most of today's diseases cannot be cured by drugs: it is only their symptoms which are controlled.

We must, therefore, look to ourselves rather than to physicians to find answers to our health problems. Given a chance the 'wisdom of the body' will usually make a better job of it than the most capable GP.

This is not to say medical treatment has no place in a health care programme. On the contrary: during the acute stage of an illness, symptomatic treatment is essential. Once this stage has passed, however, we must take a long, careful look at ourselves and our lifestyle and ask, 'Why did I become unwell in the first place?'

A useful analogy is to think of yourself as an onion with many layers — intellectual, emotional, physical and spiritual — all interacting with your surroundings through what you say and do. For a religious person this spiritual layer may be God, Buddha, Allah or some other deity, depending on their faith. To others it might be the world which lies beyond normal perception and is yet unknown. Some have experienced this world subjectively, others rely on faith, many reject the concept entirely or have decided to suspend judgement.

This way of viewing ourselves as a trinity of mind, body and spirit is termed 'holistic'. Interestingly the original meaning of *health* is 'whole'.

Managing Stress

As already explained, homoeostatic balance is maintained by the co-operative efforts of the two branches of the autonomic nervous system — the energy-expending sympathetic branch and the energy-conserving parasympathetic branch. In hyper-arousal the sympathetic branch remains in the ascendant. To combat its effects, therefore, we must find ways of increasing the strength of the parasympathetic branch. By doing so we shall neutralize the anger juice noradrenaline with a substance called *acetylcholine*, produced at the ends of the parasympathetic nerve fibres.

In the following chapters we are going to explain how this can be achieved by managing stress creatively.

This means avoiding not stress but *dis*tress in life by mastering some easily acquired skills and changing maladaptive attitudes towards life.

If you are a Type A, we would not attempt to transform you into a Type B – even supposing such a transformation were possible. But it is perfectly possible to become a healthy Type A, and so enjoy either prevention – or a full recovery – from heart disease.

THE SKILLS YOU MUST MASTER

Creative stress management demands the ability to approach life in a flexible, adaptive manner. To roll with the punches, as it were, in order that your homoeostatic 'elastic band' never becomes overstretched and your inner state variables – blood pressure, heart rate and so on – remain within safe limits.

THE TEN COMMANDMENTS OF STRESS MANAGEMENT

In her book *Fighting Heart Disease*, Dr Chandra Patel uses an alliteration based on the letter A as a way of impressing on the mind what she considers the Ten Commandments for safeguarding your heart.

These offer an excellent guide to the areas of your life where new skills or changes in lifestyle, attitude, belief or outlook may be needed. Her Ten Commandments are:

- Awareness – of the stresses in your life.
- Anticipation – to prevent needless stress.
- Action – to cope with stress.
- Avoidance – of stressful situations.
- Appraisal – of life's challenges.
- Amnesty – to reduce negative emotions.
- Assertiveness – to avoid confrontation.
- Anger management – to protect the heart.
- Altering perspectives – to remain calm.

- Assisted relaxation – to abolish tensions.

Now let's consider each of these in detail:

Awareness
This refers to the fact that until you become aware of the early signs of stress in yourself, you are obviously in no position to control it. Inscribed above the entrance to the Temple of Apollo at Delphi was one of the simplest, yet most profound, commands for a healthy lifestyle: 'Know Thyself'.

Knowing yourself confers the ability to identify and manage stress at an early stage. It means the difference between fighting a small fire in, say, an ashtray and waiting until the whole building is in flames. The first can be put out easily and effortlessly. The latter demands the attention of professional fire fighters.

Anticipation
This means being prepared for unavoidable stress. By rehearsing situations which you know will be difficult and challenging, the level of threat can be reduced, so making fewer demands on your stress bank reserves.

Action
Action involves putting coping strategies into effect so as to bring about significant changes, as necessary, in your approach to life. To hark back to our analogy of the fire in an ashtray: if one stood and watched the leaping flames without making any attempt to put them out, the fire would quickly get out of control. Merely being aware of the danger and anticipating the likely consequences would not save you from the blaze. Sadly, even when people recognize damaging levels of stress they tend to remain inactive or take inappro-

priate actions. A recent study involving several hundred men and women found that, while 72 per cent of males and 40 per cent of females admitted to feeling chronically stressed, few altered their lifestyles as a result. In fact the most likely consequence was to ask their GP for tranquillizers or drink more alcohol.

Avoidance
This consists of eliminating needless stress through careful planning and positive action. We can compare our capacity for coping with stress to money in the bank. Each time we pay out to meet a stress demand our funds become depleted. If we allow ourselves to become chronically overdrawn on the stress account, physical health is affected.

Appraisal
This commandment draws attention to the fact that our perception of events is as much a part of the stress involved as the activity itself. We view the present in the light of past experience in order to predict the future. A person stressed by public speaking, for instance, will appraise the need to make a presentation before a large audience as a considerable threat. Based, perhaps, on unhappy experiences in the past, he will approach the task convinced that failure once again stares him in the face. As a result of this appraisal there will be considerable increases in arousal and substantial demands made on his stress fighting reserves.

If, however, he enjoys public speaking, the challenge will be appraised not as a threat but an opportunity to excel. Then any slight nervousness will be viewed as pleasurable anticipation and the low level of arousal will serve to enhance rather than inhibit his performance.

Amnesty
This involves a willingness to forgive and forget, to stop harbouring grievances or holding grudges and so do away with old angers. Ruminating on past insults and reworking negative incidents from the past usually harms nobody but yourself.

Assertiveness
This is one of the most important social skills we can master. It means saying what you think and feel in a calm, direct and honest manner in order to safeguard your own legitimate rights while, at the same time, respecting the rights of others. The basis of assertive behaviour is confidence, self-esteem and the ability to communicate in a relaxed and honest manner.

Anger management
This involves replacing impulsive, maladaptive responses with a calmer and more self-assured approach. This generally requires a combination of physical relaxation, assertiveness and the restructuring of mental attitudes.

Altering perspectives
This commandment refers to changing unhelpful aspects of Type A behaviour, especially those concerned with time management and responding to set-backs and frustrations.

Assisted relaxation
What is involved here is learning basic procedures for releasing tensions from mind and body. We will be describing a practical training programme for acquiring such life-saving skills in Chapter 9.

In the next chapter we shall be looking at each of the Ten Commandments and providing practical methods for bringing about necessary changes in your life.

7

DEVELOPING AWARENESS
III Action Chapter III

The starting-point for changing the way you perceive, respond to and cope with stress is to discover exactly when, where, how and why situations arise which trigger arousal and lead to a noradrenaline assault on your heart.

You can do this by keeping a stress diary, with entries made as soon after each stressful event as possible. Such a diary is the only reliable way of monitoring the events of a busy lifestyle.

For Type As, this record is extremely helpful since the pace and pressure of their lives makes them far less conscious of any stress they are suffering at the time it arises. Usually the first symptoms are only noticed at the end of the day as they attempt to relax and unwind.

It is then, not in the heat of the moment, that such feelings as depression, exhaustion, irritability or anger, often accompanied by tension headaches, aching back or shoulders or upset stomach, begin to make their presence felt.

While you may find diary keeping a slightly tedious chore on occasions, the insights a conscientiously maintained record provides make the effort well worthwhile. Collecting this information is the essential starting-point for creative stress management.

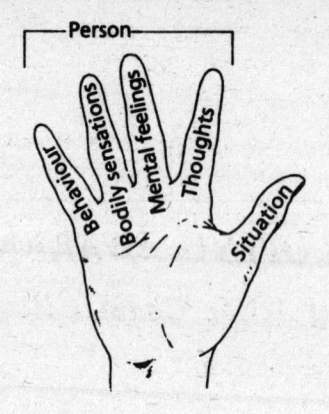

Figure 11 The five fingers of stress.

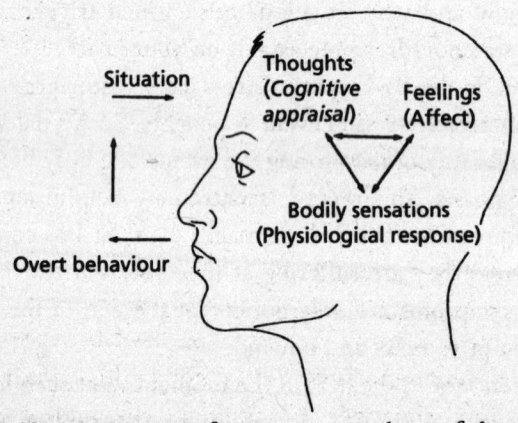

Figure 12 Our perception of stress varies according to feelings, thoughts and bodily sensations. This produces a unique individual response to the situation.

RECORDING YOUR STRESS RESPONSES
The stress response is made up of five related factors:
1 The situation you are in.
2 Your thoughts about that situation.

3 Your feelings about that situation.
4 Your bodily response to that situation.
5 Your behaviour in that situation.

Remember that this response is personal and unique. What makes one person highly stressed may leave another relaxed and happy. Your peak performance stress levels might significantly disrupt another's life.

KEEPING YOUR STRESS DIARY
This diary has three purposes:

1 To help you identify situations most likely to trigger hyperarousal and so increase levels of noradrenaline, adrenaline, cortisol and blood lipids.
2 To monitor your thoughts, feelings, bodily and behavioural responses.
3 To evaluate these objectively by assigning each a number.

What to Do – Week One

Copy, or photocopy, the sample diary page on page 97. This shows you what notes must be kept during week one. Each day, complete as many sheets as you need to record every stressful event encountered. During this time, while avoiding any situations which you will find upsetting, continue to behave as usual. The first week is intended to provide baseline data against which later improvements can be assessed.

SITUATION
This means where you were at the time, for instance in the car, office or living-room. Be as precise as possible, since you

may discover that a certain environment makes a stressful encounter more or less likely. Include a note of . . .

- Who else was present.
- What they were doing.
- What you were doing.
- When it happened.
- Where it happened.

TIME
The time is important because you may find yourself becoming more stressed at some particular hour of the day. One woman, for example, discovered she always became tense around 6 o'clock in the evening. This alerted her to the fact that it was the prospect of her husband coming home (he usually arrived just after six) which triggered a stress response.

FEELINGS
Here we mean everything experienced, whether ideas, emotions, bodily sensations, worries and so on, in an arousing situation. Rate these on a scale of 1–7, where 1 = mildly upset and 7 = very distressed.

WE RESPOND DIFFERENTLY
Some people respond to stress by becoming anxious, edgy, jittery or angry without noticing much by way of bodily arousal. Others react more physically, with increased heart rate, dry mouth, tightening of their muscles, sweating or upset stomach. Yet others feel reasonably calm and experience few disturbing bodily sensations yet have extremely negative thoughts. Our responses can also vary according to the situation. Confronting one type of challenge we may

STRESS DIARY – WEEK ONE

Day:	Date:	Time:	Situation:	Feelings:	Intensity of feelings:

have powerful feelings, in another strong bodily reactions while in a third our mind will be filled with disturbing ideas. Finally there are people who respond to stress by behaving in a particular way, when confronting any situations which distress them. They either walk away from a challenge or refuse to confront it in the first place.

For many people, their response to stress is a mixture of all four. Psychologists say they are responding *affectively*, *physiologically*, *cognitively* and *behaviourally*.

A diary entry by somebody who was mainly an affective responder might read as follows:

Stress diary – week one

Day: 1
Date: 6 May
Time: 10.25
Situation: In the office. Wondering how on earth I can fit in all my appointments. Aware of noise of typewriters and phones. Two secretaries typing and assistant at filing cabinets. Manager asks me to complete an urgent report by lunchtime. I try to explain it is impossible but my objections are dismissed.
Feelings: Overwhelming fear of failure. Feeling I am losing control over events. Swept by wave of anger and resentment which I dare not show.
Intensity of feelings: 6

A diary entry made by someone whose main responses were primarily physical reads as follows:

Stress diary – week one

Day: 3
Date: 2 February
Time: 7.35
Situation: At home with family. Daughter asks to go to party and stay out very late. My wife agrees but I say she must be home by 11 o'clock. We have a bad row.
Feelings: Heart racing, Sweating, stomach churning, mouth dry. Feel sick and faint. Afterwards have a bad headache.
Intensity of feelings: 6

Somebody whose response to stress is primarily cognitive makes the following entry:

Stress diary – week one

Day: 5
Date: 4 June
Time: 11.45
Situation: Making presentation to clients. Speaking and showing slides. One of the clients is extremely critical and attacks my ideas.
Feelings: Suddenly think my ideas probably are not much good and he is right. Complete loss of confidence. Cannot think how to respond effectively. Mind goes blank.
Intensity of feelings: 4

Finally, entries for a person whose response was to behave in a particular manner read like this:

> **Stress diary – week one**
>
> **Day:** 4
> **Date:** 9 March
> **Time:** 9.35
> **Situation:** Going into shop to return faulty electrical goods. Assistant was rude and unhelpful. Made me feel foolish in front of other customers.
> **Feelings:** Shouted at her then almost ran out of the store. Felt foolish and weak for not having stayed and stood my ground but overwhelming desire was to get away.
> **Intensity of feelings:** 6

Remember to take the notes down as soon after the event as possible while everything is still fresh in your mind.

Action

Keep the stress diary for one week starting from today.

Analysing the Stress Diary

You have now obtained valuable baseline information about the situations in which you feel especially stressed. Analyse these to see whether any particular pattern emerges. You can do this by answering the following questions:

1 *Are certain days more stressful than others?*

If the answer is *yes*, then consider what is causing this additional stress. Do you get more wound up immediately before going away for the weekend, perhaps because you try to get everything completed before the break?

Is Monday the worst for you? Studies suggest that there

is a high incidence of heart disease first thing in the week as people settle back into their work routine after two days away.

2 *Are certain times of the day more stressful?*
The peak period for heart attacks is between 7 and 11 o'clock in the morning as people prepare for the working day. Often they have to deal with a hectic rush at home, as the family competes for the bathroom and breakfast, a stressful journey into work and getting down to the labours of the morning.

3 *Are certain situations more stressful? What makes you most upset? Is it dealing with aggressive people, trying to meet urgent deadlines, being held up in traffic or forced to wait in a queue; bad service or what?*
Make a list of the most stressful events — use the values recorded under *Intensity of feelings* to assist you identify these — under appropriate headings. For example:

(i) Handling complaints.
(ii) Deadlines.
(iii) Workloads.
(iv) Unrealistic expectations of others.
(v) Being let down.
(vi) Being taken for granted, etc.

From the second week onward you can move from keeping records to thinking about ways in which the most stressful events identified may be countered through a change in the way you think about them.

This will involve making entries under two additional headings: *Thoughts* and *Challenging negative thoughts*.

THOUGHTS

Ask yourself: 'What am I thinking about in these situations which is making me feel upset?'

Writing down disturbing thoughts not only makes them easier to cope with but also gives you a better idea of how to change negative ideas for more positive ones. You will be further increasing awareness of those situations which upset you and the thoughts associated with them. It is these thoughts which are generating the mental and physical tensions which threaten your health.

Here is an example of a typical entry for the second week.

Stress diary – week two

Day: 11
Date: 9 March
Time: 3.45
Situation: Working on urgent costings in my office and constantly interrupted by colleague who keeps coming in with queries he could perfectly well answer for himself.
Feelings: Anger at his lack of consideration, worry about not meeting my deadline. Felt temper rising at each interruption. Heart beating more rapidly.
Thoughts: He's deliberately trying to sabotage my efforts. He dislikes me and wants to prevent me succeeding at this job. He's trying to undermine my confidence.

Once again it is important to make your notes as soon after the event as possible. Be as thorough as possible when recording your thoughts, even if these seem irrelevant or irrational once the incident has passed.

CHALLENGING NEGATIVE THOUGHTS

This can be done by changing your perspective on the situation and considering whether there might not be alternative ways of explaining, or dealing with, what is happening to you.

Here are three diary entries made by clients which illustrate how negative thoughts can be challenged.

> ## Stress diary
>
> **Day:** 12
> **Date:** 2 March
> **Time:** 8.45 a.m.
> **Situation:** Stuck in traffic jam on way to important appointment.
> **Feelings:** Fury at other drivers responsible for delay and making me late.
> **Thoughts:** I am going to miss the appointment and the client will be angry. I may miss the sale and it is all the fault of these fools. They are deliberately driving slowly to annoy me. I was a fool not to realize how bad the traffic is and start earlier. It's my fault.
> **Challenging the thought:** I will probably make it on time. Even if I am a few minutes late it won't be the end of the world. Everybody knows rush hour traffic is terrible. Why make matters worse by working myself up into a state? I am only hurting myself.
> **Stress level:** 5

Stress diary

Day: 18
Date: 11 October
Time: 4.15 p.m.
Situation: Disciplining a subordinate for poor time-keeping in my own office. No one else present.
Feelings: Angry with him for putting me into this unpleasant situation. I sound unassertive, weak and ineffectual. Heart racing, sweating and feel slightly sick. Have to keep hands in lap so he can't see they are shaking. Sound curt and unsympathetic.
Thoughts: He's probably laughing at me behind my back. Will tell the whole office what a wimp I am. Worry about being unfair and how he will respond to my criticisms. Fear he may become abusive or aggressive.
Challenging the thought: It's my job to discipline subordinates. He's brought this on himself. If he gets upset that's his problem. It's unlikely he is laughing behind my back, but if he wants to react that way, that's his problem too.
Stress level: 4

Stress diary

Day: 22
Date: 23 February
Time: 9.15
Situation: In crowded bar of hotel after a long and tiring train journey. No room service so have to get

> sandwiches at counter. Crowded and only two people serving. Waited 10 minutes but was constantly ignored by staff.
> **Feelings:** Already irritated by lack of room service. Angry at being treated with such poor service. Desire to hurt or punish them in some way for ignoring me.
> **Thoughts:** How dare they not notice me and take my order. I'll be rude when they do serve me and tell them just what I think of them. They are doing it deliberately because I am not a regular or perhaps they think I look unimportant. I'll demand to see the manager.
> **Challenge the thought:** They are busy and badly staffed. It's unlikely you are being ignored deliberately, and even if you are, getting worked up won't help. Don't stay here again. Having a row won't do any good.
> **Stress level:** 4

You will have noticed an additional change in the diary forms from the second week onward. Instead of noting down *Intensity of feelings* from now on we want you to evaluate the level of stress experienced using the following scale. Depending on the situation you may feel some, or all, of the responses listed below.

STRESS SCALE

Score 1: *Relaxed and confident*.
Well able to cope with the situation without feeling uncomfortably aroused. Pleasurable anticipation. Mild excitement.

Score 2: *Some discomfort*.
A desire to avoid the situation. Wishing it had never happened. Mild physical discomfort, i.e. butterflies in the stomach. Sense of irritation or niggling frustration.

Score 3: *Moderately angry or anxious.*
Some loss of confidence. Doubts about meeting the challenge. Uncomfortable bodily sensations such as rapidly beating heart, dry mouth, etc., sweating. Feeling you are getting wound up. Tension in the muscles. Desire to get your own back for some imagined wrong or slight. Sense of being unfairly treated.

Score 4: *Strong emotional and/or bodily response.*
Loss of temper leading to angry outburst. Shouting at the other person. Desire to hurt or upset them. Thoughts: 'I can't cope' or 'I must escape', 'How dare they', 'I'm going to get even for this.'

Score 5: *Overwhelming response.*
Extreme anger, rage, guilt, fear, disgust, etc. Control over emotions is lost as you lash out in fury or panic.

Muscles are tense, heart beats rapidly. Feel cold and clammy or very hot. Sweating profusely. Stomach cramped. Feel weak and exhausted immediately afterwards.

KEEPING YOUR DIARY

As before complete these sheets as soon after each incident as possible.

When challenging your negative thoughts, act like a prosecuting lawyer and demand proof for each statement. Ask yourself:

- How do I know this is so?
- What evidence is there to support this view of the situation?
- Even if it is true, does it really matter?

As well as situations which arouse disagreeable feelings of

stress, you should also note down pleasant activities. When doing so you need only challenge any thoughts which are negative. For example:

Stress diary

Day: 26
Date: 8 July
Time: 4.20
Situation: Presenting ideas to colleagues at informal gathering – 15 others present.
Feelings: Positive and confident. Relaxed. Performed well and got over all the points I wanted.
Thoughts: Clear-headed and decisive. But worry I may really be boring them but they are too polite to say so. Are they criticizing me behind my back?
Challenging the thought: There was no evidence I bored them: quite the contrary. If they are being critical behind my back all I can do is anticipate and answer such criticisms.
Stress level: 3

It is important to include situations where the stress produced positive responses, since these indicate areas of your life where you are currently functioning at your PPSL. They can also serve as a warning that stress levels are rising, since we often find it harder to undertake challenges which once came easily, when becoming increasingly worn down by stress. Indeed having difficulty, or finding no pleasure, in tasks once tackled with ease or found pleasurable is a good indication of impending burn-out.

To summarize the stress diary:

Week one – Situations. Feelings. Intensity of feelings. This is to obtain baseline data.

Week two – Situations, Feelings. Thoughts. Challenging negative thoughts. Stress level.

From week two onward note also any positive situations which you regard as a challenge.

By the start of the second week you will have a clearer idea of the situations which are damagingly stressful and this will make it easier to get in touch with your thoughts.

Charting your Stress

From week two onward, we want you to plot your daily stress levels on a chart like the one illustrated below.

		Morning	Afternoon	Evening
Stress	1 Green			
Level	2			
	3 Amber			
	4			
	5 Red			

As you will see, we are using the same colour coding as on the questionnaire in Chapter 3. Arousal in the green is helpful to performance.

Amber alerts you that stress levels are rising and should be brought back under control.

Red is for danger and *distress*. You are using up your stress-combating reserves too rapidly. If this continues there is a risk of burning out.

The purpose of producing such a chart is to help you iden-

STRESS DIARY – WEEK THREE ONWARD

Day:	Date:	Time:

Situation:

Feelings:

Thoughts:

Challenging negative thoughts:

Stress level:

tify any stress 'hot spots' in your day. That is, days when you seem to become more vulnerable to negative feelings and emotions.

Anniversaries of some unhappy events, such as a bereavement, for instance, can make an otherwise normal day highly stressful. Indeed, so powerful can this reaction prove, that if you ever experience a profound mood change or raised levels of stress on a particular day it's worth trying to recall if anything traumatic ever happened to you either on that day or at that time of year.

We are highly sensitive to subtle environmental clues, such as the first flowers of spring, smell of the sea, birdsong, colours, textures or some feature of a person's appearance. These can trigger a powerful emotional response which may lead to a sudden loss of confidence, anxiety, anger or depression. A likely explanation for taking an instant dislike to somebody at first meeting is that they remind us of someone who was upsetting or hurtful.

A particular month may prove more stressful than all the others. April, for example, which poet T. S. Eliot described as 'the cruellest month', really does seem to live up to his grim observation, since it sees the greatest number of suicides and admissions to mental hospitals. This is caused by the regular biorhythm of our body clocks, which respond both to times of day and seasons of the year.

Your diary and chart will help you pinpoint all these normally overlooked elements of creative stress management.

8

CHANGE YOUR MIND – TO SAVE YOUR HEART

III Action Chapter III

Like most of the remaining Ten Commandments for safeguarding your heart, the second of them, anticipation, becomes easier to practise once you have the accurate record of stressful situations your diary provides.

Anticipation

By anticipating your likely reaction to stressful situations you can rehearse more positive coping strategies. For instance, recognizing that you find confrontations difficult to handle, yet also knowing some are unavoidable, you might work out an approach which minimizes your levels of arousal during such encounters. This may be by using some of the other skills we shall discuss later, such as changing your perception of the event from one in which confrontation is inevitable to one in which a measure of co-operation is possible. Reappraising situations is often a good way of recasting the roles you have assigned other people and rethinking former tactics.

Equally you might decide that greater assertiveness or improved anger management was necessary so as to reduce the degree of confrontation experienced. Assisted relaxation and constructive fantasy, both of which are taught in the next chapter, will enable you to remain physically and mentally calmer during potentially stressful encounters.

ANTICIPATION AND LIFE EVENTS

While some kinds of stress occur so unexpectedly that anticipation and planning prove impossible, many life events, even those which involve significant changes and demand considerable readjustment, can be predicted well in advance, for instance, children growing up and leaving home or our retirement from work. Other coming events cast shorter shadows before them, but may still allow time for preparation, for instance, moving home; the ending of an important relationship; the illness of a loved one; redundancy or, especially, bereavement.

Career changes are, not surprisingly, especially stressful to Type A individuals since their work is often central to self-identity and self-esteem.

The secret of controlling stress in all these events is anticipation and planning. Start as early as possible because time has a habit of slipping past with remarkable speed.

Instead of allowing retirement to creep up on you almost unawares, for example, prepare well in advance for all the changes this will bring about.

Dealing with unexpected changes, e.g. the end of a relationship you believed to be secure or the death of a loved one, is usually far trickier since the stresses created by significant loss, whether through parting or bereavement, are amongst the most painful and powerful emotions we can experience. Never feel embarrassed about showing your feelings. Holding back tears is a barrier to psychological health, not a sign of inner strength. Crying and grieving are safety valves with life-preserving values.

It is natural – and necessary – to pass through various stages of grieving. These typically start with denial: an instinctive reaction to being given bad news is to gasp, 'Oh no. . . .'.

Next comes guilt as you bitterly reproach yourself with thoughts such as: 'If only I had behaved differently this might never have happened', followed closely by anger directed towards the other person with thoughts like: 'How could he cause me such pain?'

Once the first shock has passed, however, it is essential to stop brooding about what might have been and start searching for any positive features in the change. While these may be very hard to find on occasions, there is often at least one glimmer of comfort or hope even in the most tragic circumstances.

Review whatever options have been opened up to you by the change in terms of your overall goals in life, and seek to replace what has been lost by activities which offer equal, even if very different, levels of stimulation and gratification.

Control and health

The greater control you can exert over events, the easier it will be to maintain your peak performance stress level and so safeguard your health. There are two reasons why this should be so. First, knowing that you can influence what is going to happen reduces anxiety and increases self-confidence. This enhances the enthusiasm and determination with which life's challenges are approached, so helping to set up a self-fulfilling prophecy of success.

Secondly, controlling events means it is far easier to bring about changes in the working or home environment that will reduce or eliminate needless sources of stress.

There will, of course, be occasions when control is

snatched from your grasp so suddenly and unexpectedly that there is little you can do, at that moment, to influence events. Accept that when this happens, through accident or misfortune, you will experience a significant increase in stress. The essential thing is to regain as much control as possible as swiftly as you can. Where possible seek help, comfort and advice from family and friends. But don't allow this short-term, healthy, need for social support develop into a longer-term dependency. Once the immediate crisis is over, it is essential to reassert your independence and take responsibility for your life.

Often control slips from one's grasp gradually, as the result of several minor incidents rather than a single major catastrophe. This usually occurs when a vicious circle develops between loss of control and increases in stress levels.

Something happens that makes it harder for you to control events. As stress undermines confidence and performance, your loss of control increases. This raises levels of anxiety, impairs motivation and undermines self-esteem, leading to a steeper decline in performance and further loss of control.

The answer is to keep a watchful eye on your ability to control events and resist any proposals – however well-intentioned – that lessen your freedom of action.

Action

In Chapter 1 we explored some of the reasons why people who have suffered a heart attack are often very reluctant to take any positive steps to improve their chances of recovery. Avoidance and denial of reality are, as we explained there, powerful psychological defence mechanisms designed to

Panic

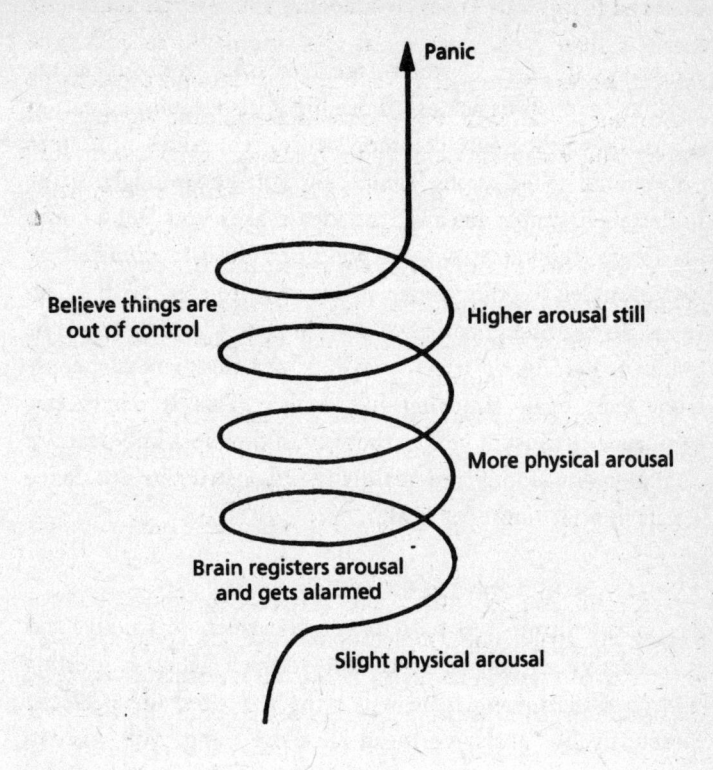

Believe things are out of control

Higher arousal still

More physical arousal

Brain registers arousal and gets alarmed

Slight physical arousal

Figure 13 As anxiety rises motivation and performance decline sharply.

reduce distressing anxiety. Yet unless you are prepared to put the procedures we describe into practice, little or no improvement is likely. Be action-orientated. Take the initiative to bring about these important changes in your life. Remember that if you do what you've always done you'll get what you've always got.

As parachutists say – It won't mean a thing if you don't pull the string!'

Avoidance

Avoiding situations which are stressful without doing anything to help us achieve those life goals established earlier is not cowardice but common sense. This does not mean you should avoid doing something you know ought to be undertaken simply because the idea makes you feel anxious or upset. The more we postpone or refuse to confront an important issue, the harder it becomes to deal with effectively. In the first chapter we described how avoidance of the issue of their heart attack prevents vast numbers of people from ever again enjoying full health. This is destructive avoidance because it gets in the way of the most important of all life goals – a long and healthy life! Constructive avoidance assists in your quest for health.

AVOIDANCE AND LIFE GOALS

The simple litmus test to determine between destructive and constructive avoidance is to ask yourself whether dealing with that distressing issue will bring a desired life goal any closer. By life goals we mean all those things you wish to achieve in the key areas of family, social, career and leisure.

An effective, if slightly macabre, way of establishing life goals is to write your own obituary! Not as it would be should you die tomorrow, but as you would, ideally, like it to read. Use the form overleaf to direct you but then be as imaginative as you like. The purpose of creating such a fantasy obituary is to concentrate one's mind on major life goals. That done, it becomes far easier to decide what practical steps need to be taken to accomplish them. For instance:

Peter died last night aged 110 and in perfect health right up to the end in his luxurious home on a romantic Pacific island. Peter worked as a consultant achieving the position of managing director. Outside his work Peter's chief interests were his wife and children with whom he had a warm relationship. His hobbies included scuba diving, sailing and swimming. Peter's many achievements included giving generously to charity and helping to support many worthwhile causes. He will be best remembered for his friendship, generosity and good company.

_____ died last night aged _____
(Your name)   (the age you'd like to be)
in _____
(where you would most enjoy living)
_____ worked as a _____
(Your name)   (The career you'd most like to follow)
achieving the position of _____
                              (where you hope to rise)
Outside his/her work _____ 's chief interests
                              (your name)
were _____
_____
(the hobbies, leisure activities, interests you have or would like to follow)
_____ 's many achievements included _____
(Your name)
_____
(what you hope to accomplish)
S/he will be remembered for _____
_____
(all you have or would wish to achieve)

Having completed the obituary, ask yourself what you are doing to turn those dreams into reality. Peter, for instance, might consider whether he is safeguarding his health by watching his diet, taking more exercise and controlling his hostility. Is he working to acquire new management skills, spending enough time with his family, taking up a sport and so on?

Think where you would like to be and what you would hope to have achieved in each of these time periods: short term (1–12 months); medium term (2–5 years) and long term (5 years plus).

Having established life goals, you can check whether avoidance is positive or negative by deciding whether a particular action will help accomplish them. If the honest answer is *yes*, then tackle it – perhaps using one of the other procedures we teach, such as assertiveness or assisted relaxation, before doing so. If it does not advance you along the road chosen, then avoid it because you'll be paying a high price for something of absolutely no value to you.

Appraisal

Before his heart attack Alex became terribly upset over what he now recognizes were trifles.

> *I would get into furious arguments over what seemed like valid reasons at the time. But looking back I am amazed that I allowed myself to become so worked up. I still get into similar situations to before my heart attack, only I no longer fly off the handle. The world hasn't changed. My attitude has.*

Alex's comment echoes those made by many who come back successfully from a heart attack. Their outlook changes with the result that life's challenges are appraised entirely differently.

The idea that by shifting one's viewpoint you change your whole attitude towards events has its origins in antiquity.

OUR WINDOW OF BELIEFS

In AD 60 the Roman writer Epictetus commented: 'Man is disturbed not by things but the views he takes of them.' Shakespeare echoed the same thought when he made Hamlet say: 'There is nothing either good or bad, but thinking makes it so.' Similarly the poet Alexander Pope wrote: 'All seems infected to th' infected spy, as all looks yellow to the jaundiced eye.' Writer Paul Dubois put it like this in 1905: 'If we wish to change the sentiments it is necessary before all to modify the idea which produced them.'

Alfred Adler, an early disciple of Freud, wrote: 'It is very obvious that we are influenced not by "facts" but by our interpretation of them.' George Kelly, an influential American psychologist, stated that events are only meaningful in relation to the ways they are viewed by each individual. He wrote:

> *Reality does not reveal itself to us directly, but rather it is open to as many alternative ways of construing it as we ourselves invent . . . all our present perceptions are open to question and reconsideration . . . even the most obvious occurrences of everyday life might appear utterly transformed if we were inventive enough to construe them differently.*

Events do not, as George Kelly put it, carry their meanings 'engraved on their backs' but have any significance imposed on them by the way different individuals interpret them.

Recall that stress results from an interaction between the individual and the situation in which he finds himself. It is your perception of events, rather than the events themselves, which lead to heart-damaging hyperarousal.

In making sense of a complex and confusing world we each develop a set of beliefs (Kelly called them *constructs*). Some of these beliefs we may hold so dearly that they are never questioned and we might be willing to die rather than change them. Religious or patriotic beliefs often come into this category. Other beliefs are held less firmly and we might be perfectly willing to change them in the face of evidence to the contrary. You might believe, for instance, that your neighbour is an honest person. But having read a report of his arrest for robbery, you immediately – and without suffering any distress – believe him to be dishonest. On the other hand if it was your son rather than a neighbour who had been charged with robbery, that change in your belief system would be a lot more difficult, and painful, to accept.

Beliefs are not merely the window through which we look out on the world. They also determine how we behave and respond to others. An executive might believe, for example, that the only way he could ensure respect and obedience was by being a 'hard' man and behaving in an aggressive, intolerant and distrustful manner. On most occasions his 'theory' works well. Others treat him respectfully and, even if only out of fear, obey him.

Then he meets somebody who is indifferent to his aggression, shows him little respect and does not obey his orders. At first he will become angrier, less tolerant and more suspicious – just as a child whose whimpered protests are ignored will escalate his protests into a full-blown temper tantrum. When this strategy still fails to produce the expected result and if that person is important to him or exercises influence over him, the aggressive businessman may eventually change his belief system and adopt a gentler, more tolerant and trusting approach.

Most of our strongest and least easily altered beliefs are

formed during childhood as a result of the way parents and other influential grown-ups like teachers, relatives, etc., expected us to behave. Once established, they provide the window through which we evaluate experiences. These are so basic to our view of the world that we seldom question or challenge them. They appear to provide not merely the best way of coping with life but the only way.

Even when events show them to be unhelpful or even downright harmful, we tend to cling to them rather than reassess our outlook on life.

Usually believing one thing about a person means we automatically hold several related beliefs at the same time. We might believe, for example, that successful people are always happy, or that intelligent people are always going to be emotionally cold.

DILEMMAS, TRAPS AND SNAGS
By combining in various ways, our beliefs determine how we perceive life's challenges. Psychiatrist Dr Anthony Ryle calls three of the most important 'dilemmas, traps and snags'.

A dilemma occurs when two or more beliefs are tied in such a way that accepting one means you will inevitably either accept or reject another. For example, a man might believe: '*If* I am a good and dutiful son *then* I must always do what my parents expect of me.'

Should he find himself in a situation where he fails to meet his parents' expectations, this man will probably feel stressed by the belief he is no longer a good son.

The second kind of dilemma, where one belief excludes another, would arise if a woman believed, for example: '*Either* I am totally selfless and only do what my husband wants *or* I am selfish and disloyal.'

A wife who held these beliefs about marriage might feel

extremely stressed, anxious and guilty if she wanted to become more independent and do the things she had always wanted to do rather than passively agreeing with her partner's demands.

Traps occur when two people in a relationship have dilemmas which reinforce one another. In the case of the woman who believed that she would be disloyal if she thought more about her own wants and needs, for example, her partner might believe: '*If* my wife really loves me *then* she will always fall in with my wishes.'

Here the woman's quest for independence would make her husband believe she no longer loved him as much. He might then behave less lovingly towards her, so confirming her belief that she could only expect to be loved so long as she was unquestioningly dutiful. Breaking free from traps is often difficult and painful.

Snags are defined by Tony Ryle as 'subtle negative aspects of goals': they are the sort of beliefs which usually start with the phrase 'Yes, but...':

'Yes, but I believe if I stop being aggressive people are going to walk all over me.'

'Yes, but I believe unless I have lots of stimulation in my life it is simply not worth living.'

Therapy has been described as a means for discovering how to talk to yourself in a more helpful and adaptive way. In order to come back from a heart attack – or reduce the risk of having one in the first place – it is very important to explore and, where necessary, review your beliefs.

Entries in your stress diary may prove extremely helpful identifying possible dilemmas, traps or snags. Review any events that upset you, together with your thoughts about that situation. Now ask:

'What beliefs influenced my response to that situation?'
'How might my response have changed if my beliefs were altered?'

Examine the beliefs underlying your response to those events and then challenge them as you did your thoughts in the stress diary. For example, a common dilemma arises from the belief: '*Either* I must be loved or approved of by every person in my life *or* I am diminished as a human being.' When challenged, this might be replaced by the more realistic view that: 'While it's nice to have people like and admire you even without that I can still accept and respect myself.'

If you detect an *if . . . then* dilemma such as: '*If* successful *then* always having to race from one task to the next' or an *either . . . or* dilemma like: '*Either* achieving perfection in all I do *or* a total failure', try adopting a less constricting set of beliefs.

This could be: 'It is perfectly possible to be successful without always racing against the clock' or 'Making mistakes does not mean I am a failure.'

Be on your guard for traps and discuss these whenever possible with your partner, or whoever else is involved in sustaining an unhelpful and unhealthy pattern of mutual beliefs.

Finally move from the snag-centred 'Yes, but. . .' response to certain challenges to a 'Yes and . . .' outlook.

'Yes and then I could try . . .'
'Yes and then we might . . .'

For the person trapped by 'Yes, but . . .' the world is filled with impossibilities. For those who say: 'Yes and . . .' it becomes full of possibilities.

THE DANGER OF BEING TOO PERFECT

Be especially careful of any dilemmas which place a high premium on perfection such as: '*If* not 100 per cent successful in all I do, *then* a worthless person' or '*Either* constantly achieving *or* a complete failure.'

These perfectionist beliefs are usually acquired very early in life and generate significant levels of unhealthy stress and unhappiness. 'My father was never satisfied with anything I did at school,' a client told one of us (David Lewis). 'If I came second in class he demanded to know why I hadn't come first. All my adult life I have been trying to be as perfect as possible in order to please a man who died when I was 15.'

Instead of being motivated by a strong need for achievement, in which one constantly seeks new challenges and learns from mistakes, the driving force for a perfectionist is often a potent fear of failure. The desire, at almost any cost, never to make misjudgements, errors or blunders.

Perfectionism is one of the problems most often encountered in therapy. When people find themselves unable to match their unrealistic self-expectations they feel depressed and threatened. 'Pushing for perfectionism may not be the winning strategy you think it is,' says psychiatrist Dr David Burns of the University of Pennsylvania Medical Centre. 'Each perfectionist thinks it can help make for a better performance, when actually it cripples the person with procrastination, emotional misery and insecurity.' In a study of more than 700 men and women, Dr Burns found nothing to suggest that perfectionists did any better, socially, financially or personally, than non-perfectionists.

Amnesty

'Forgive your enemies,' advises the Bible. It's sound advice for ensuring a healthy heart. Unfortunately giving up old grudges, abandoning long-held grievances and learning to forgive and forget is often very hard. Many people have belief systems which link forgiveness with weakness and not holding a grudge with allowing others to take advantage of you. For instance '*If* I allow people to put one over on me *then* I shall be seen as spineless' or '*Either* I am hard and unforgiving *or* I shall be trampled on.'

The problem is that hostility usually triggers a hostile response from others, which makes you feel more threatened and therefore more aggressive in turn. In the words of C. H. Cooley:

Each to each a looking glass,
Reflects the other that does pass.

To feel less hostile and experience less hostility one must start behaving in a less hostile manner. Return to the stress diary and see if there were any occasions when you said or did something in order to get your own back and put the other person down, to make him feel bad because he had made you feel bad.

Now ask yourself: 'Was I in the wrong?'

Continue to question all beliefs which cause you to feel angry, bitter, rejected or in any other way hostile either to a specific individual or the world in general. Do this several times each day, whether or not you actually believe yourself to be in error. By constantly questioning our beliefs we are able to eliminate many unhelpful and unhealthy assumptions.

Show greater affection and admiration for those you work

with, for your partner and children. Make a point of responding sensitively to any tenderness towards you. Remember anniversaries, buy unexpected gifts, do small kindnesses – they'll bring in big rewards. Do not assume that somebody 'knows' you love, respect or admire them. People are not mind-readers, although we often act as if they were. Everybody, even those for whom we have the most tender feelings, needs reassurance now and then, especially if a busy lifestyle allows little time together.

Make a real effort to understand and accept those you don't much like. Treat them in a more open, trusting and friendly manner and they could turn out to be a lot nicer than you imagined.

Even if your overtures are rejected – and initially they may arouse some suspicion if people are not used to your behaving in this way – you will still be the winner. Hostility is a toxin that can kill you as surely, if not as swiftly, as a deadly poison. Eliminate it from your system by opening yourself to the love and beauty around you.

Assertiveness

By assertiveness we mean defending your legitimate rights as an individual. It does not mean attacking another's equally legitimate rights: that constitutes aggression.

Many people have difficulty being assertive because they become so anxious when attempting to stand up for themselves. As a result they have only two responses – docile compliance or outbursts of anger.

The assisted relaxation described in the next chapter will help banish the handicapping symptoms of anxiety, so making it easier to remain assertive during confrontations.

Consider whether you have any beliefs which may limit

your ability to act assertively, for instance: '*If* I stand up for myself *then* people are going to reject me' or '*Either* I agree to whatever other people want *or* they will dislike me.'

Challenge these beliefs. For instance, you may have to accept that if you are more assertive some people may indeed not act in quite such a friendly way towards you. But see that as more their problem than your own. They cannot be very self-assured if unable to remain friendly with somebody who stands up for his or her rights. Ask yourself whether you really want to buy their good opinion at the price of your independence.

Stop appraising situations in terms of extremes. There is usually a middle way between perpetually giving in or being unreasonably selfish.

Use constructive fantasy, described in the next chapter, for rehearsing situations where you want to be more assertive. It will help you present your views calmly but firmly in previously stressful encounters. Start by working on those situations, identified in your stress diary, where assertiveness would have proved healthier and more helpful than meek compliance.

Anger Management

Not long ago one of our patients was kept waiting in a bank to cash a cheque:

> *There was a long queue and I was short of time. Suddenly I felt my anger, and my stress, rising. Only one teller and six unmanned places, how stupid. Look at that silly customer chatting away. There's no service these days. Where are they all? Probably at the back drinking tea. . .'*

Such silent monologues turn feelings of irritation to annoyance, annoyance to anger and — if allowed to continue — anger to blind rage. It's what is meant by the expression 'talking yourself into a fury'.

During uncontrollable anger, blood vessels in the retina can buckle, shift and swell to a point where the sufferer really does 'see red'. It is a stage where anger can easily turn to hatred. The Greek philosopher Aristotle wrote more than 2,400 years ago:

> *The angry man feels pain, but the hater does not . . . Much may happen to make the angry man pity those who offend him, but the hater under no circumstances wishes to pity a man whom he has once hated; the angry man would have the offenders suffer for what they have done; the hater would have them cease to exist.*

'Driving into work during the rush hour makes me hate the other motorists,' a client confessed. 'It's not just anger; it is pure loathing.'

'I dream about having machine guns fitted to the front of my car and being able to blast them out of existence.'

It's a fantasy many share, judging by the commercial success of a little electronic gadget designed to produce a variety of blood-curdling sounds, such as the boom of cannon fire and the zing of lasers. The manufacturers claim that by fitting it to a dashboard it gives the frustrated motorist a chance to let off steam. A more likely consequence, however, is that it will merely encourage feelings of boiling rage in a situation where the only person to be hurt is the angry driver him- or herself.

If you feel yourself getting angry, try this quick way of winding down:

- Tell yourself *'Stop'*. Firmly but silently.
- Take a deep breath then exhale slowly. While doing so allow your shoulders to sag and relax your hands.
- Breathe in again. Exhale and make sure your jaw is relaxed, teeth parted and your tongue is loose in the bottom of your mouth.
- Breathe in and out again, three more times.
- Think about the pleasant, relaxing scene used during the constructive fantasy training which we shall describe in the next chapter.

Altering Perspectives

As we have explained it is the degree of rush and hurry, so typical of the Type A, which creates much of the frustration, anger and hostility felt whenever deadlines or work schedules are threatened. An important element in altering perspectives is to manage time more efficiently so as to minimize conflicts arising through over-commitment.

Assign priorities to your major activities according to their importance in helping you to achieve life goals. This makes it easier to respond to different demands on your time. When faced with any task there are only four ways of responding.

You can . . .

- Drop it.
- Delay it.
- Delegate it.
- Do it.

DROP IT
This sounds easy, but breaking well-established patterns of time-wasting behaviour usually demands determination and self-discipline.

We slip so easily into a habit of doing certain things, there is almost a sense of loss and deprivation when the routine is broken. Take reading junk mail. Many people devote several minutes each week to wading through unsolicited mail. If this serves one of your major life goals then it should be continued. More often, however, such an activity uses up time which might more usefully be devoted to a genuine goal, such as talking to your family or partner across the breakfast table, reflecting on problems at work, planning a holiday and so on.

DELAY IT

Delaying can be a time-waster, when it involves procrastination. This form of negative delay involves replacing a high priority activity with one of much lower priority.

Instead of settling down to prepare an urgent report you waste time on the low priority task of tidying your filing system or sharpening all your pencils!

Positive delay is involved when . . .

- You postpone a low priority task for one with a high priority.
- You postpone a task which arouses strong emotions, such as anger, depression, bitterness or envy.

  Suppose, for example, you are angry with a client and decide to write him a rude letter. A letter which, once you have calmed down again, would probably never be written and certainly not sent. By delaying you not only spare yourself needless stress at the time, but avoid becoming even more stressed during the angry confrontation which is likely to result after he has read your note.
- You have insufficient information or lack the requisite amount of skill to undertake the task efficiently. A great

deal of unnecessary stress is caused by people making faulty decisions on the basis of partial or inaccurate information. Type As, being more attracted by action than reflection, tend to respond impulsively and often land themselves in stressful situations as a result. The old saying 'If you want a quick answer, it's no!' often makes excellent business sense. Before reaching any conclusions step back and ask yourself whether you really have *all* the knowledge needed to make an informed and rational decision.

- Your physical or mental state are such that it seems unlikely you could carry out the job successfully. Decisions reached while overtired or the worse for drink are seldom sound and frequently a cause for regret later on.

DELEGATE IT

Effective delegation is one of the greatest time-savers there is, and something many Type As find it extremely hard to do efficiently. Not only does it allow you to assign more time to tasks which only you can perform, it probably means you'll get a better job done all round. Anticipate situations in which you can delegate successfully.

DO IT

This is the stage where some people come unstuck. Although they have clearly identified a high priority job, they can never find the right moment to begin. As a result they leave things too late and have to rush to complete the task on time, so increasing their levels of stress.

It's a good idea to make your final chore each evening planning and preparing for the next day's tasks. Set aside time for routine tasks and those you simply can't avoid. If possible begin with the more demanding tasks and leave the easier ones until later in the day: that way you'll be investing your energy more efficiently.

Your time management plan must be sufficiently flexible to cope with the unexpected. The unscheduled meeting, the surprise visit from an important client, the party invitation which comes out of the blue, a last-minute panic at work, and so on.

This is where setting yourself clearly defined goals proves so helpful by making it far easier to decide which tasks should be dropped, delayed or delegated.

LAUGHTER REALLY IS THE BEST MEDICINE

Alter your perspective by taking life less seriously and trying to see the funny side of situations more often. Humour also helps you control anger and become more assertive. Whenever we laugh vigorously our whole body is given a brisk workout. Shaking with mirth transforms us into a living vibrator, massaging heart, diaphragm and thorax. Rapid breathing means more oxygen-rich blood to the cells. During laughter air is sucked into the trachea at up to 70 mph, cleansing it of mucus, clearing out foreign matter and helping prevent bacteria from multiplying.

Laughing also brings about electrochemical changes, releasing hormones and brain transmitters which improve mood and lift the spirits. Laughing may stimulate the pituitary gland, increasing output of the body's natural pain killers, endorphins and enkephalins.

By distracting our mind from sad thoughts or everyday worries, laughter relieves boredom and reduces tension.

In Sweden Dr Lars Ljungahl organizes 'laughter' therapy for patients suffering from depression and finds it reduces the symptoms. 'Laughter may be an antagonist to the classical stress response,' says immunologist Dr Lee Berk.

Dr William Fry, Associate Professor of Psychiatry at Stanford University Medical School, and an expert on the physiological effects of laughter, considers humour 'one of the best strategies for maintaining good health'.

Laughter can also be used to defuse anger. Rather than work yourself into a fury over a set-back or frustration, attempt to find something amusing in what has happened. Imagining an assertive individual stark naked will often help you feel less intimidated.

But not all laughter has equal value. Mechanical guffaws, for example, are less effective in sustaining good health than a sense of humour which allows you to find amusement in everyday situations and enjoy a keen sense of the ridiculous.

THE TENTH COMMANDMENT
So far we have looked at nine of our heart-saving ten commandments. In the next chapter we will explain how to master the tenth and in some ways most vital — assisted relaxation.

9

THE RELAXATION RESPONSE
III Action Chapter III

Relaxation is a natural antidote to stress, since it is impossible to be both relaxed and stressed at the same time. By strengthening the 'slow down' (parasympathetic) branch of the autonomic nervous system (ANS), assisted relaxation allows you to exert control over the sympathetic branch when it seeks, unhelpfully, to increase arousal.

Bidding farewell to needless physical tension is the essential first step to enjoying peace of mind.

For some people, bodily relaxation automatically brings about mental tranquillity. For others, freeing themselves of physical tension is insufficient to ensure inner calm. Their body is relaxed but their mind remains tense.

In our 21-day assisted relaxation programme we shall be explaining how to control stress in both mind and body.

Learning Assisted Relaxation

There are many different ways of learning to relax, but the procedures we describe have been found to work rapidly and effectively in the vast majority of cases.

Try to practise twice a day, for around 15 minutes at a time, over the three-week period.

Before starting, take note of the following points.

CHOOSING YOUR SURROUNDINGS

The room selected for assisted relaxation training should be one in which you already feel calm and secure. For many this is the bedroom, while others favour the lounge. You may find that different types of decor exert an influence over your ability to relax. Blues and greens, for instance, are known to be so psychologically soothing that, for many people, just being in a room decorated with these colours proves relaxing. Subjects placed in such surroundings during research studies were found to have lower blood pressure, reduced heart rate, slowed respiration and a calmer state of mind. Red, by contrast, acts directly on the speed-up branch of the ANS, producing increased physical arousal. This is why red has always been associated with warnings and danger.

Drab colours such as dark browns, creams and other institutional colours make some people feel rather depressed. If you are among them, avoid such surroundings during relaxation training. The choice of colour is such a personal matter we can only suggest you experiment, so far as is possible, with different types of decor.

The room chosen should be as quiet as possible and you must be able to remain undisturbed throughout the session. Take the telephone off the hook and hang a 'Do Not Disturb' sign on the door.

Because you will be lying still for quite a long time, it's important that the room is comfortably warm before you start.

DECIDING ON POSITION

Some people like to lie on a bed or sofa while relaxing, others prefer sitting in a comfortable armchair. Experiment with different positions until you find the one in which you can unwind and let go most easily. Make certain your lower back is fully supported, perhaps by placing a small cushion between the back of the seat and your lumbar region.

If lying down . . .

Lie flat with a small pillow supporting your head. Your head should be straight on the pillow and not turned to either side. Have your arms outstretched at your side, not touching the body, with palms facing downward.

Your legs should be outstretched, slightly apart, with feet flopping outward in a 'ten to two' position.

Make yourself as comfortable and symmetrical as possible. If you suffer back problems you may be more comfortable with a pillow under the knees.

If sitting down . . .

Sit right back in the seat so that your back is well supported. Let your thighs flop out into an open position. Your knees should not be too sharply bent. The angle at the knees must be slightly greater than 90° with your feet flat on the floor. If your thighs are rather on the short side, add some extra support by placing a small pillow behind your back. Place your hands palm down on your thighs or on the armrest of the chair. If there is no support for your head, allow it to be held centrally on the neck. In this position the head is balanced on the cervical spine and a minimum amount of muscular effort is required to hold it there.

In either position carry out the following check before starting to relax.

Do I feel comfortable and balanced?

Repeat this question several times, starting at your feet and working upwards to legs, body, neck, shoulders, arms, forehead, eyes, mouth and jaw.

WHAT TO WEAR

While there is no need for any special clothing, avoid anything too tight or constricting. Remove your shoes and loosen or remove tight clothing before you begin. Something warm but loose-fitting, such as a tracksuit, is ideal.

LIGHTING

Some people find it easier to concentrate when lying in a slightly darkened room, while others find this stressful. One option favoured by many is to fit a table lamp with a dimmer switch, available from any electrical store. They can then adjust the level of illumination to suit their particular mood on that day.

TIME OF DAY

Biorhythms have a powerful influence over levels of arousal. *Bodytime* author, Gay Gaer Luce, comments:

> *Most people don't realize how much they change over 24 hours. They may notice that they get particularly tired at 2 a.m., or chilly late in the evening . . . [However] they remain largely unaware of changing immunity to infection or stress [which drops at night] or the fact that blood pressure, mood, pulse, respiration, blood sugar levels . . . and our ability to handle drugs all rise and fall in a circadian rhythm.*

Even childbirth follows a pattern: most babies arrive between midnight and 6 a.m. When averaged out, mood changes reveal a pattern with cycles as long as three to six months. Our body temperature rises by around half a degree in the first three hours after we awake and this period is associated with the most consistent improvements in efficiency found throughout the day.

Dr Karl Klein of the Institute for Flight Medicine in Bad Godesberg, Germany, found that the intellectual skills of volunteers peaked from one hour after noon to seven in the evening. Physical strength and stamina were greatest, and they obtained best results when tested for reaction times and motor co-ordination skills. The worst results were obtained between 2 and 6 a.m.

Our brain's spontaneous production of alpha waves – electrical patterns associated with mental relaxation – also varies at different times of day and night. Continuous monitoring of brainwaves has revealed that both the frequency and the amplitude of these waves change from one hour to the next.

We suggest you begin by choosing any convenient time of the day to practise relaxation. Most people find that when they arrive home from work and then immediately before going to bed are the most suitable times. They have the additional advantages of helping you to wind down after a stressful day, so enjoying a more relaxed evening, and to get a better night's rest. But if you find it hard to relax at these times, try shifting your sessions around.

DIRECTION
During your early training sessions, try facing in different directions to see whether this makes relaxation easier or harder to achieve. For reasons which are far from clear, some people find relaxation much easier to achieve if they sit or lie along, say, the North–South axis. Others favour an East–West orientation or any points on the compass between.

MUSIC

Many people prefer to have some light background music while relaxing. This prevents the silence becoming too oppressive and also helps safeguard them from being disturbed by sudden, unexpected noises from outside the room. Avoid music which triggers strong emotions, even when these are positive. Tunes that bring to mind a time when you were especially happy, for instance, can prove as distracting as those arousing feelings of sadness.

Both work against the state of passive alertness which we wish to achieve by evoking a host of powerful, distracting recollections.

Some researchers have found that the music of Mozart, especially, has the ability to aid the co-ordination of breathing, cardiovascular and brainwave rhythm, producing positive effects on health.

American music therapist, Steve Halpern, talks of 'sound nutrition'. He says that it feeds the body, 'massages our organs, changes hormone levels, reduces stress, and increases the capacity for learning'.

Of special value in relaxation training is Baroque music, composed during early decades of the eighteenth century onwards and including such composers as Handel, Bach, Telemann, Corelli and Vivaldi. The last of these composers has a wonderfully soothing effect on babies, and will often send a fretful baby to sleep.

A possible explanation for such music's unique ability to induce a tranquil mental state may be found in its structure. Eighteenth-century composers sought to create an ideal form and harmony in their music so as to achieve a unity of sound that would release the mind from worldly cares. They introduced contrasts between movements, between the treble melody and the bass accompaniment, as well as between instruments. Mendelssohn once commented: 'Music cannot be expressed in words, not because it is vague but because it is more precise than words.'

In their quest for harmony, the Baroque composers created music whose frequency is precisely tuned to generate a state of relaxed awareness in the brain. Experiment with different types of classical music from this period to discover whether any particular piece enhances your relaxation training sessions.

THE HEALING BREATH

Before reading further try this simple test. Place one hand on your stomach and the other on your chest. Breathe normally and notice which one rises and falls.

If it is the hand on your abdomen, you are breathing correctly and abdominally by using the full capacity of your lungs.

Should your chest hand rise, however, your breathing is too shallow. This increases the risk of hyperventilation in situations where you become stressed.

THE HAZARDS OF HYPERVENTILATION

The range and variety of symptoms produced by hyperventilation are seldom realized. Sufferers, who are often considered neurotic, may complain of some or all of the following: palpitations; dizziness; faintness or blackouts; acute anxiety; 'unreal' feelings; inability to concentrate; exhaustion and impaired intellectual performance; disturbed sleep; nightmares; and sweating.

Hyperventilation is able to produce this devastating effect because it removes too much carbon dioxide from the system, with the result that all the bodily fluids become more alkaline. This leads to a reduction of up to 40 per cent in coronary blood flow, as blood vessels constrict.

In addition, carbon dioxide has a greater affinity to the red blood cells, so the amount of oxygen being delivered to the tissues decreases. There may also be a release of catecholamines, causing the blood platelets to clump together and leading to a greater risk of thrombosis. Irregular heart beats can be triggered due to effects on electrical conductivity. The rate at which signals travel through the nervous system is accelerated and the 'slow down' branch of the ANS is depressed, leading to greater sympathetic arousal.

Habitual unstable breathing is primarily a matter of bad habits – excessive sighing, sniffing, nervous cough – which often run in families. It is also more common among Type A men, especially those with a tendency to be perfectionist. The first attacks of hyperventilation often follow a physical illness and having a general anaesthetic can prove a potent trigger.

During the training programme we shall show you how to control your breathing so as to avoid the damaging and distressing effects of hyperventilation.

EATING, DRINKING AND SMOKING

As we shall explain in the next chapter, caffeine in tea or coffee and nicotine in cigarettes are potent stimulants and so should be avoided for at least an hour prior to relaxation training. It is a good idea to relax on a full stomach, since you are already more relaxed by the process of digesting food.

One final tip. Be sure to empty your bladder before starting the session!

BE PREPARED FOR INITIAL DIFFICULTIES

When they start relaxing people sometimes find themselves tensing up again. This is perfectly normal.

What happens is that as you notice your muscles becoming less tense, you either become pleased – 'It's starting to work!' – or apprehensive – 'Will I stay relaxed?'

Both thoughts increase arousal, so jerking you out of a state of relaxation.

A second reason is that needless muscular tension can become such a habit we are not normally even aware of being stressed. As the stress vanishes its absence feels strange, unnatural and even a little worrying.

Do not feel concerned if you experience this see-sawing of tension and relaxation during your early practice sessions. They will disappear once you become more familiar with the feeling of deep relaxation.

A second problem for many is intrusive thoughts. As you begin to feel calm and peaceful a disturbing thought pops unbidden into your mind. You start to worry about what is going to happen, fret over an irritating problem at work or even find your mind filled with mundane ideas about what is showing on television.

Should this happen to you, neither dwell on the thought nor attempt to fight it. Simply notice the idea in a passive way before returning your attention to the business of relaxation. By adopting this approach you should find the intrusive thought quickly disappears. Later in the programme we shall be providing other ways of dealing with such distractions.

The 21-Day Programme

Follow this programme carefully and resist the temptation to skip ahead or start using more advanced procedures too early.

Once you have mastered relaxation, the skill can be used in any situation where handicapping arousal is experienced or anticipated. It enables you to control the response of mind and body in such a way as to maintain your peak performance stress level in all normal everyday situations.

Even if you have experienced anxiety and stress in the past, relaxation should allow you to approach challenges more calmly and confidently than ever before.

But remember that, as with any skill, you need to practise regularly in order to achieve a consistent measure of success. If you have got into the habit of becoming afraid or angry during particular encounters or in certain kinds of situation these feelings may, at first, be too strong for your relaxation response to overcome entirely. Persevere, however, because you will get there in the end.

Complete the notes on each relaxation sheet so that you have a full record of your training.

Monitor the level of physical – and, later in the programme, mental – relaxation achieved on a scale of 1–5 as follows:

1 Remained physically and mentally tense throughout.
2 Relaxation achieved for brief moments.
3 Fairly relaxed for the whole session.
4 Deeply relaxed for most of the session.
5 Very deeply relaxed throughout.

HOW TO USE THE PROGRAMME
Read the notes for each day's training over several times until you fully understand the procedure and need not disturb your relaxation by referring back to them. However, if you do forget what to do next, the summary, printed in bold, will jog your memory quickly and easily.

Day 1   Tick the box on completion
Time started............. Time finished.................
Music (if used) ....
Level of relaxation achieved............................

What to do – Day 1

Close your eyes lightly and feel yourself sinking more deeply into the chair or bed.

Pay attention to the rhythm of your breathing and as you breathe in notice your chest and abdomen rising a little, while as you breathe out your chest and abdomen will fall a little. When you are relaxed you will find that your breathing becomes slower, shallower and smoother. As you exhale, feel the tension flowing from your body with the expelled air, leaving you a little more calm and relaxed with each exhalation. Breathe in and out continuously with no pause between inhaling and exhaling, so that the air flows constantly and effortlessly into and out of your lungs. Each time you breathe out repeat the word 'calm' silently to yourself.

The secret of success in relaxation is *passive concentration*. That is, focusing the mind on what is happening without trying to make it happen. There must be no striving or compulsion to attain a relaxed state. The harder you try, the more tense you will become.

Now, starting at your toes, start to notice any needless stress in different parts of your body. Inside every muscle are special nerve endings which monitor levels of tension and report this information to the brain. When under chronic strain, however, their messages tend to be ignored.

The purpose of these early exercises in assisted relaxation is to help you begin paying attention to these important signals once again.

Move slowly up your body, focusing attention on each part of the body in turn.

Wiggle your toes then let them remain still. Notice the difference between these two states. Rotate your ankles, then relax them and, once again, notice any differences.

Now attend to the muscles in your calves and thighs. Feel these becoming warmer and heavier.

Proceed to the muscles in your buttocks, lower back and hips. Imagine these too becoming more and more deeply relaxed, warmer and heavier. Each time you breathe out imagine a little more tension flowing away from these major muscle groups.

Notice the muscles of your abdomen and chest. Release any tensions here. Allow your tummy muscles to flop right out.

Moving to your upper back and shoulders, let yourself sink even more deeply into the chair or bed. Sag your shoulders and imagine the tension flowing away from them.

Wiggle your fingers and rotate your wrists a couple of times. Notice, as before, the different sensations when moving and motionless.

Finally concentrate on the muscles of your face. The desire to conceal our emotions, mentioned earlier, makes these among the hardest groups of muscles to relax fully.

Smooth out your brow, let your jaw hang loose with teeth slightly apart and tongue resting limply in your mouth. Your eyelids should rest gently together. Feel all these muscles growing warmer and more relaxed. Keep your breathing slow and regular, and each time you breathe out feel yourself becoming more and more deeply relaxed.

End the first part of this session by opening your eyes, taking one deep breath and flexing your muscles.

But do not get up from the chair or bed. Having aroused

yourself, go through all the exercises again. Repeat three times this first session. When you have finished stand up slowly or you may feel slightly giddy. Try and carry the sensation of relaxation into your everyday routine.

What to do – Day 1
- **Breathe continuously – no pause between inhaling and exhaling.**
- **As you breathe out feel your body becoming warmer and heavier.**
- **Each time you exhale repeat the word 'calm' silently to yourself.**

Day 2   Tick the box on completion ☐
Time started............. Time finished.................
Music (if used) ....
Level of relaxation achieved.............................

What to do – Day 2
Return to the same position as Day 1. This time, however, you are going to deliberately tense and then relax the muscles in your arms so as to train yourself to become more aware of the difference between tension and relaxation.

Spend the first few minutes calming yourself down by repeating the exercise described on Day 1. Breathe slowly but continuously and, each time you exhale, repeat the word 'calm' silently to yourself. Feel all your tensions flowing away with each exhaled breath and notice that your body is becoming warmer and heavier.

Now start by tensing the first group of muscles – those in the forearm, the extensors and the flexors. If seated, make sure your wrists are resting on your thighs.

Tense the first of these by extending the hands at the

wrists. Bend your hands back, raising them from the bed or chair and feel tension in the back of the forearm. You will also notice a feeling of strain at the wrist.

Hold this position for a slow count to five. Now relax, let your hand flop down. Do not lower it gently.

Feel the tension flowing out of them and notice the difference between tension and relaxation in these muscles.

Now tense your flexors by reversing the movement: that is, flexing your hand at the wrist.

Hold the forearm tension as before for a slow count to five. Then flop your hands back onto the chair or bed.

The next set of muscles to work on are those in the upper arms, the biceps and the triceps.

Tense the biceps by attempting to touch the *back* of your wrists to your shoulders.

Press back and feel tension increasing in the front of the upper arms. Hold for a slow count to five. As before let your arms flop limply back onto the bed or chair. Do not lower them slowly.

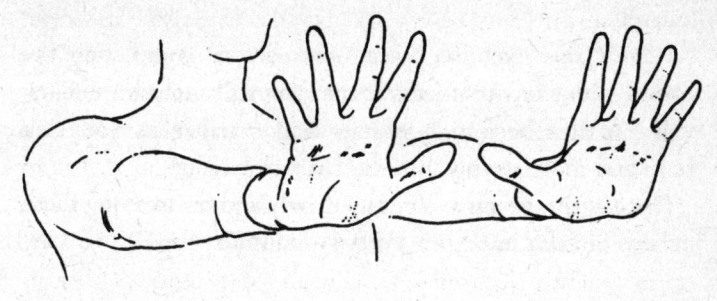

Figure 14 Deliberately tensing the extensor muscles in order to relax them.

Now tense the muscle in the back of the upper arm, the triceps, by stretching your arms out as straight as possible. Hold for a slow count to five and relax yet again.

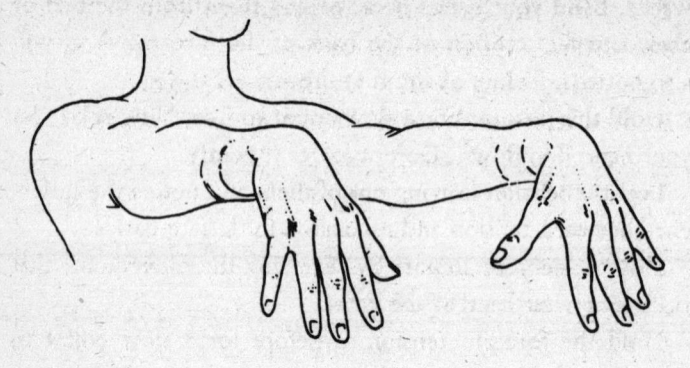

Figure 15 Deliberately tensing the flexor muscles in order to relax them.

Let your arms flop down by your side and feel the tension leaving these muscles as your arms become heavier and warmer.

Focus these feelings of deep relaxation in your hands and arms. Keep the flow of your breathing continuous and, each time you exhale, repeat the word 'calm' silently to yourself.

Repeat this exercise twice more before completing the session with a few moments spent lying still and calm, feeling your muscles becoming heavier and warmer as you sink more and more deeply into the chair or bed.

Once again, be sure to get up slowly and try carrying these feelings of calm into your everyday routine.

What to do – Day 2
Deliberately tense the muscles of your arms by:
- **Raising your hands at the wrists – let them go limp.**
- **Bending your hands at the wrists – let them go limp.**

- **Touching the back of your wrists to your shoulders – let them go limp.**
- **Stretching your arms – let them go limp.**
- **Repeat the word 'calm' each time you exhale.**

Day 3 Tick the box on completion
Time started............. Time finished.................
Music (if used) ....
Level of relaxation achieved ....

What to do – Day 3

Start as on the two previous occasions by spending a couple of minutes becoming more relaxed and feeling yourself sinking more deeply into the chair or bed. Feel all your muscles becoming heavier and warmer as the tensions flow away from your body. Each time you breathe out repeat the word 'calm' silently to yourself. Breathe continuously so that there is no interruption to the flow of air into and out of your lungs.

Today you will be concentrating on relaxing the muscles in your face and neck. These are often under so much needless tension they can prove among the hardest to relax. However, with practice you will be able to smooth away all the strain.

First tense and relax the muscles of your arms and hands following the same procedures described on Days 1 and 2. Hold for a count to five, then let your hands and arms flop limply down. Imagine all your tensions flowing out of the fingertips and away into the room, never to return.

Now you are ready to tense the muscles of the face and neck.

Start with your frontalis muscle in the forehead. Tense this by raising your eyebrows and wrinkling your forehead. Hold the tension for 5 seconds then relax. Smooth out your forehead and notice the difference between tension and relaxation in these muscles.

Now lower your eyebrows and, by frowning, tense the corrugator muscles. Feel the build-up of tension between your eyebrows just above the bridge of the nose.

Hold, as before, for a slow count to five, then relax by smoothing out your brow.

The next groups of muscles to tense are those in your throat and jaw.

Do this by clenching your teeth hard while pressing the tip of your tongue against the roof of the mouth. Hold for a slow count to five.

Now relax. Let your jaw hang loose with teeth parted and your tongue resting in the bottom of your mouth. Once again focus on the difference between tension and relaxation in these muscles.

Turn your attention to the muscles around your eyes. Tense these by screwing up your eyes. Hold for a count of five and release. Your eyelids should rest lightly together, with no tension in the muscles.

Breathe continuously, silently repeating the word 'calm' with each expelled breath. Feel the muscles of throat and face becoming more and more deeply relaxed.

Tense the muscles in your neck by pressing back as hard as possible against the chair or bed. Press and hold for the slow count to five. Relax, allow your head to rest lightly against the support.

Finally, tense the muscles in your shoulders by hunching them as high as you can. Hold this tension, as before, for a slow count to five. Let them drop limply and feel all the tension draining away from your neck, face and shoulders.

Deepen this sensation by focusing on the word 'calm' and

imagining all the stress being expelled from these muscles with each exhaled breath.

Repeat these actions three times before completing the training session, as on previous occasions, by spending a few minutes focusing on all your muscles and feeling them becoming warmer and heavier.

Remember to get up slowly and try to carry these feelings of deep relaxation into your everyday activities.

What to do – Day 3
Deliberately tense the muscles of your arms by:
- **Raising your hands at the wrists – let them go limp.**
- **Bending your hands at the wrists – let them go limp.**
- **Touching the back of your wrists to your shoulders – let them go limp.**
- **Stretching your arms – let them go limp.**
- **Open your eyes wide as though enquiring – smooth out your brow.**
- **Frown deeply – smooth out your brow.**
- **Screw up your eyes – rest them lightly together.**
- **Press the tip of your tongue to the roof of the mouth – let your tongue rest loosely in your mouth.**
- **Clench your teeth tightly – let the jaw relax.**
- **Press your head back against the support.**
- **Hunch your shoulders hard – let them sag loosely.**
- **Repeat the word 'calm' each time you exhale.**

Day 4 Tick the box on completion	☐
Time started............. Time finished.................	
Music (if used)	
Level of relaxation achieved............................	

What to do – Day 4

The additional muscles to tense and relax today are those of the chest. Go through the same procedure as on previous days. Spend a few minutes calming down and focusing on your breathing. Each time you exhale repeat the word 'calm' silently and imagine yourself becoming more and more deeply relaxed. Your muscles are becoming heavier and warmer as you sink more and more deeply into the chair or bed.

Tense the muscles of your hands, arms, face and neck together. Increase the tension for a slow count to five, then let go. Flop out completely and feel the stress and tension flowing away from your hands, arms, shoulders and head.

Now deliberately tense the muscles of your chest by taking and holding a deep breath. Inhale until the chest cannot expand any further. Hold this tension for a count of five. Exhale and, as you do, feel all the stress and tension flowing away from your body.

Repeat the exercise a total of three times. Complete the session by focusing on all your muscles and imagining them becoming warmer and heavier.

Be careful not to get up too quickly when finished and try carrying these feelings of relaxation into your everyday life.

What to do – Day 4

- **Tense the muscles of your upper and lower arms.**
- **Open your eyes wide as though enquiring – smooth out your brow.**

- **Frown deeply – smooth out your brow.**
- **Screw up your eyes – rest them lightly together.**
- **Press the tip of your tongue to the roof of the mouth – let your tongue rest loosely in your mouth.**
- **Clench your teeth tightly – relax your jaw.**
- **Press your head back against the support. Hunch your shoulders hard – let them sag loosely.**
- **Tense the chest by taking and holding a deep breath – relax and breathe continuously again.**
- **Repeat the word 'calm' each time you exhale.**

> **Day 5** Tick the box on completion
> Time started............. Time finished.................
> Music (if used) ....
> Level of relaxation achieved.............................

What to do – Day 5
Proceed exactly as before but today add another group of muscles to the exercise.

These are the muscles of the abdomen. Having tensed and relaxed all the other muscles, tense these by flattening your stomach as though expecting a blow. Pull the muscles in hard. Hold for five seconds and relax. Let your tummy muscles flop right out. No stress or tension in any part of your torso, face, neck, shoulders, arms or hands.

Repeat three times and complete by feeling the sensation of relaxation spreading throughout your body.

What to do – Day 5
- **Deliberately tense the muscles of your arms, face and chest.**
- **Tense your stomach muscles by flattening them as though expecting a blow.**

- **Breathe continuously and repeat the word 'calm' silently to yourself each time you exhale.**

Day 6 Tick the box on completion ☐
Time started............. Time finished.................
Music (if used) ....
Level of relaxation achieved............................

What to do – Day 6
Proceed as on previous days by tensing and relaxing each of the muscle groups dealt with so far. Now add the final group, the muscles in your legs and feet.

Tense these by stretching the legs as hard as you can and pointing to your toes. Before doing this exercise proceed as on previous days, first by unwinding generally, then by tensing and relaxing all the other groups of muscles.

Hold the tension for five seconds then relax completely. Sink back into the chair or bed and feel all your tension flowing away. Each time you breathe out silently repeat the word 'calm'. Focus on the absence of tension throughout these major muscle groups. Continue breathing quietly and continuously. Repeat the word 'calm' on every exhaled breath.

As you say this silently to yourself imagine the sense of deep peace filling your whole being.

What to do – Day 6
- **Deliberately tense the muscles of your arms, face, chest and stomach.**
- **Tense your leg muscles by stretching them and pointing your toes.**

Day 7 Tick the box on completion	
Time started............. Time finished................. Music (if used) .... Level of relaxation achieved............................	

What to do – Day 7
Lie quietly, feeling yourself becoming warmer and heavier. Breathe continuously. Each time you exhale, feel more and more tension flowing away from your body.

Tense and relax *all* your muscles in turn as on the previous days. Repeat three times with a rest period of around one minute between each session.

Complete the training period by spending several minutes focusing on the very relaxed state of your muscles. Imagine your whole body is warm and heavy and repeat the word 'calm' to yourself as you exhale.

What to do – Day 7
- **In turn tense muscles in your arms, face, chest, stomach and legs.**
- **Breathe continuously and repeat the word 'calm' silently to yourself each time you exhale.**

Day 8 Tick the box on completion	
Time started............. Time finished................. Music (if used) .... Level of relaxation achieved............................	

What to do – Day 8
Today you will learn how to develop a tranquil state of mind by means of a procedure we call *constructive fantasy*.

Start by tensing and relaxing all your muscles using the

procedure taught in the first week. Feel your body becoming warmer and heavier. Keep your breathing continuous so there is no pause between inhalation and exhalation. Each time you breathe out repeat the word 'calm' silently to yourself.

When you feel physically relaxed, you can start training your mind to unwind and banish remaining tensions.

You achieve this by mentally picturing yourself transported to some very quiet, secure and peaceful setting.

This can be a beautiful garden, some tranquil country scene or a sunny seashore. You may even prefer to imagine yourself at home in a comfortable chair.

It doesn't matter which location you choose, so long as your imaginary surroundings make you feel contented, secure and at peace.

This place in the mind will become your private sanctuary from the hustle and bustle of the world. A haven where you feel no stress or tensions and there is only beauty.

Perhaps you will paint a scene in your mind's eye of blue skies, the sun shining, beautiful flowers or a calm sea gently lapping the golden sands of a desert island. You can return to this very special haven any time you feel stressed.

Imagine the scene as vividly as possible. Not only seeing your surroundings, but hearing and feeling them as well.

If you picture yourself lying on a sunny beach, feel the hot sun on your face and the warm sand beneath your body. Hear waves unfolding onto the shore. Smell the scent of blossoms or the salty tang of the ocean. Notice a gentle, spicy breeze ruffling your hair. Spend a few minutes developing this scene and holding it in your mind. Your breathing is continuous and you silently repeat 'calm' with each exhalation. You now feel very relaxed and at peace with yourself.

There is no tension in your muscles and your mind is at

ease. Focus on these feelings and enjoy them. You are completely at peace. No stress. No tension. No anger or anxiety. You feel calm, confident and perfectly secure. Continue practising holding this scene to the end of the session.

Do not worry if, at first, you find it hard to develop a very full image or to hold that scene for very long. Distracting thoughts may intrude, the intensity of your mental picture vary, some aspects of the scene – perhaps the sounds or the image – prove easier to imagine than others. None of these need be any cause for concern since everybody has some difficulty in mastering constructive fantasy when they first begin. Practise regularly and you will find it much easier to create and sustain a vivid mental picture.

What to do – Day 8
- **Tense and relax the muscles of your arms, face, chest, stomach and legs in turn.**
- **Breathe continuously – no pause between breaths.**
- **Say the word 'calm' silently to yourself each time you exhale.**
- **Conjure up some pleasant, relaxing image.**
- **See, hear and feel your fantasy surroundings as vividly as possible.**

Day 9 Tick the box on completion
Time started............. Time finished.................
Music (if used) ....
Level of relaxation achieved.............................

What to do – Day 9
Repeat the procedures for Day 8. Practise holding the image for longer and making it more vivid.

Work on any aspects of the fantasy scene which prove difficult, for instance the sense of touch or hearing.

Day 10   Tick the box on completion
Time started.............. Time finished..................
Music (if used) ....
Level of relaxation achieved.............................

What to do – Day 10
Repeat as for Day 9. By now you should be achieving a good level of physical and mental relaxation.

Do not be concerned, however, if you still find yourself becoming slightly tense during the course of relaxation, experience distracting thoughts or have difficulties holding the mental image in constructive fantasy. With a little further practice you will find it increasingly easy to remain relaxed throughout the session, to prevent yourself being disturbed by intrusive thoughts and to sustain a strong, vivid picture of your chosen surroundings.

Try developing a passive, accepting attitude towards the training. When something happens to distract or disturb you, simply notice it in a calm detached manner and then quickly return to the training.

Day 11   Tick the box on completion
Time started.............. Time finished..................
Music (if used) ....
Level of relaxation achieved.............................

What to do – Day 11
Repeat the procedures practised on Day 10. Focus especially on your breathing, and be sure to inhale and exhale without pause so that air flows continuously into and out of your lungs.

Notice your body becoming warmer and heavier as the relaxation deepens.

Practise creating and sustaining your mental image. Add details and work especially on any aspect of the constructive fantasy, perhaps the sounds or scents, with which you have experienced any difficulties.

> **Day 12** Tick the box on completion
> Time started.............. Time finished..................
> Music (if used) ....
> Level of relaxation achieved..............................

What to do – Day 12

Repeat as before but on this occasion, before completing the session, and at a point when you feel deeply relaxed, calm, confident and secure, do the following.

Place the first two fingers of each hand on your forehead, about mid-way between your eyebrows and the hairline. You will find two small areas of raised bone ridges.

Having identified them, press gently with your fingertips and repeat the following: 'Any time I start to become angry or tense, I need only do this to feel calm and relaxed.'

Massage the skin lightly for a moment repeating the words while doing so. Now let your arms rest by your sides and spend a few moments enjoying the sensation of being deeply relaxed.

Rise slowly and go about your everyday activities calmly, carrying these feelings of relaxation into your normal routine.

> **Day 13** Tick the box on completion ☐
> Time started............. Time finished..................
> Music (if used) ....
> Level of relaxation achieved.............................

What to do – Day 13
Repeat the exercises of the previous day and continue deepening your physical relaxation while perfecting the imagery.

Apply gentle finger pressure to your forehead while giving yourself the instruction that a sense of tranquillity can be achieved very rapidly by massaging these bones.

> **Day 14** Tick the box on completion ☐
> Time started............. Time finished..................
> Music (if used) ....
> Level of relaxation achieved.............................

What to do – Day 14
Repeat as for previous day. After two weeks of training you should be able to accomplish the following without too much difficulty:

- Become physically relaxed within a few moments of sitting or lying down. Feel your body becoming warmer and heavier as the muscles unwind and lose their tension.
- Banish most of the distracting thoughts through passive concentration.
- Breathe continuously, allowing a constant flow of air to pass into and out of your lungs.
- Hold a clear mental image of your chosen haven.
- Carry some of these feelings of relaxation into your everyday life.

From today onward we want you to practise rapid relaxation in everyday situations where you start to become tense, angry or anxious. As soon as you notice signs of arousal sit quite still, close your eyes (where possible) and focus on your breathing. Breathe continuously and each time you exhale, repeat the word 'calm' to yourself. Notice each of the main muscle groups in turn and see whether there is needless tension. Are your fingers uncurled, your shoulders hanging limp and loose, your jaw unclenched, brow smooth, tongue resting on the floor of your mouth, and so on?

If you detect unhelpful tensions, imagine the muscles involved becoming warmer and warmer. You should then find yourself becoming calmer and more relaxed within a few moments.

Day 15   Tick the box on completion   ☐
Time started............. Time finished.................
Music (if used) ....
Level of relaxation achieved.............................

What to do – Day 15

Repeat as for Day 14. But from now on, in addition to relaxing whenever you start feeling aroused, anticipate situations which are likely to increase stress levels. For instance a confrontation with an angry superior, a drive through heavy traffic, and so on.

Immediately prior to any such encounters, or following an activity which has increased your stress, do the following:

Find a quiet, private place where you can sit down. Loosen any tight clothing and remove your shoes.

Sit quietly with your eyes lightly closed, the lids resting gently together. Focus on your breathing. As before ensure this flows smoothly with no pauses between inhalation and exhalation. Repeat the word 'calm' to yourself with each outward breath.

Apply two-finger massage to your forehead as instructed and allow feelings of peace and tranquillity to fill your mind. Continue for 15 seconds, then open your eyes slowly and, just as slowly, stand up and go about your everyday routine.

Day 16   Tick the box on completion   ☐
Time started.............   Time finished.................
Music (if used) ....
Level of relaxation achieved..............................

What to do – Day 16

Today you will add a new item to your increasingly powerful repertoire of procedures for controlling mental and physical tension.

This is cardiac regulation, which means the heart beat or pulsation produced anywhere in the body.

It sometimes helps to get in touch with your heart if you lie on your *left* side and place your right hand over your heart, just under the breast below the nipple area.

You should now be able to feel the heart beating, but if this proves difficult, take the pulse in your wrist.

As you become more relaxed you'll find that your heart beat slows, becomes regular and beats less forcibly. Notice this happening and, as it does, repeat silently to yourself: 'My heart beat is calm and regular.' After a little training you will find it possible to regulate your heart so that its rate of pumping becomes slower and more rhythmic on demand. Introduce cardiac regulation into all your assisted relaxation training sessions from now on.

The Relaxation Response

> **Day 17** Tick the box on completion ☐
> Time started............. Time finished.................
> Music (if used) ....
> Level of relaxation achieved............................

What to do – Day 17

This is the moment in your training to start using constructive fantasy to remain calm during arousing situations. We have already explained how these procedures can be used to reduce stress before, during and after such encounters. But where you know certain activities will make you feel stressed, you can reduce tensions experienced by rehearsing that scene in your mind's eye well in advance of the real-life event.

Use information from your stress diary to identify those situations which, typically, make you anxious or angry.

After picturing your tranquil, relaxing scene for a few moments, switch the fantasy to one of the activities selected from your stress diary.

Do not choose a challenge which makes you feel extremely aroused, since this may prove too stressful to handle, even in fantasy, at this stage of training. Instead select one which scored around 4 or 5 on the diary's 7-point stress scale.

Try to create a fantasy which includes as many features of this stress-arousing situation as possible.

- See it vividly – the colours, movement, people present, settings, etc.
- Hear it intensely – imagine what words are most likely to be spoken, by yourself and all the others present.
- Feel it – if you are sitting down in the situation, imagine the weight of your body on the chair.

Hopefully, creating this event in your mind's eye will make you emotionally aroused. Note the point at which stress levels start to rise and use these as a cue to cope in the scene.

Continue picturing yourself taking an active role in the encounter. Imagine being simultaneously alert and yet relaxed. Challenge any negative thoughts, as you did in your diary. Reappraise the situation in your imagination. Question the beliefs on which your feelings of anger or hurt are based. To what extent might you be able to change your response by altering your beliefs?

Imagine yourself coping confidently and successfully with that challenge without getting worked up.

Day 18 Tick the box on completion ☐
Time started............. Time finished.................
Music (if used) ....
Level of relaxation achieved.............................

What to do – Day 18
Repeat as for Day 17. Work on either the same challenging situation in fantasy or another chosen from your diary.

If you found yesterday's session easy, then select a rather more stressful challenge.

Day 19 Tick the box on completion ☐
Time started............. Time finished.................
Music (if used) ....
Level of relaxation achieved.............................

What to do – Day 19
Repeat as for Day 18. But add a further relaxation procedure, which can be used quickly and completely unobtrusively in any situation, at a meeting for instance, on public transport or

in any other location where it is impossible to find the privacy needed for the types of relaxation used before.

At the start of your training session, concentrate attention on your dominant hand. That is the right hand if you are right-handed, the left if left-handed. You are going to train yourself to increase the temperature in this hand by a couple of degrees. By doing so you will quickly become calmer and less aroused. This is because, as we have seen, during the fight and flight response blood is diverted away from the vessels directly beneath the skin and sent to the muscles in preparation for the anticipated burst of activity.

By consciously instructing your ANS to return blood from deep in the body to the periphery, you will automatically become more relaxed. The effect of the warm blood is, of course, to increase the temperature of your hand.

There are three main ways of warming your hand and we advise you to try all of them to find out which works best for you:

- Focus attention on your right hand and imagine heat rising from the palm and fingers. With a little practice you should gain a clear impression of increased warmth.
- Picture yourself holding the hand in front of a blazing log fire.
- Place your palm an inch away from either cheek. This is a natural hot spot and you will feel the heat against your hand. Imagine it flowing from your face and warming the hand.

This impression of the hand growing warmer is no illusion. If you use a small alcohol (not a clinical!) thermometer to measure changes you can watch the temperature rise as you will the hand to warm.

> **Day 20** Tick the box on completion ☐
> Time started.............. Time finished..................
> Music (if used) ....
> Level of relaxation achieved.............................

What to do – Day 20

Repeat all the procedures you practised on Day 19.

By now you should be fairly proficient at the following important stress management skills:

- Progressive relaxation – during which you release tension from the major muscle groups by first deliberately tensing and then relaxing them.
- Quick relaxation – carried out in real-life situations.
- Constructive fantasy – both for relaxing the mind by conjuring a soothing, relaxing scene and for carrying the feeling of calm confidence into imagined challenges.

Now add one final skill to your repertoire. This is active relaxation, which can be used to control your level of bodily arousal in everyday situations. It involves noticing and removing any unnecessary muscle tension. Here's how you do it.

At the end of a relaxation session, slowly rise but then, instead of immediately going about your everyday chores, take a little longer to focus on each of your main muscle groups in turn while walking slowly and calmly around the room.

Start by paying close attention to the muscles in your arms, wrists and hands. Do these feel needlessly tense?

Are your fingers clenched into a fist or uncurled and limp?

Are your arms taut or comfortably loose at your sides?

Have your shoulders become tense again? In other words, are they raised up towards your ears? If so, let them relax and hang like a coat hanger. Check all your muscle groups in this way, being on the lookout for any unhelpful tension and then relaxing it away.

Are you standing straight? Your spine works best and is least vulnerable to stress or injury while vertical.

Are you frowning or furrowing your brow?

Are your teeth clamped tightly together?

Is your tongue pressed up into the roof of your mouth?

Notice ways in which you are making your body tense and then relax away needless tension.

Continue to make occasional checks while performing everyday tasks. Ask yourself: 'Am I sitting, standing or lying in a way which places my muscles under tension for no good reason?'

While seated at a desk, in a train, plane or behind the driving wheel for long periods, make regular checks, since it is only too easy to increase internal stress by poor posture.

Day 21 Tick the box on completion

Time started............ Time finished................

Music (if used) ....

Level of relaxation achieved...........................

What to do – Day 21

This is the final day of formal training, but for assisted relaxation to remain an effective health-enhancing tool, you must continue using all the procedures we have described on a regular basis. From today onward make relaxation and constructive fantasy a part of your daily routine.

Relax at least once a day; perhaps just prior to going to sleep, since it will help to ensure a restful night.

Use rapid relaxation or hand warming whenever you start to feel aroused.

Prepare for any potentially stressful encounters by using constructive fantasy.

If you feel yourself getting worked up then calm down by gently massaging the two points on your forehead.

Your Stress Management Check-List

Here are 12 simple but effective ways to safeguard your health against the harmful effects of excessive stress:

1 Talk over your worries. We all need to do this from time to time because it helps us put things into perspective.
2 Escape from your problems – even a short break helps you see things more clearly.
3 Burn away tension with physical activity (see Chapter 12).
4 Give in to others now and again.
5 Do something agreeable for somebody else at least once a day. Even a smile or a kind word is a start.
6 Get your priorities sorted out and deal with one thing at a time.
7 Avoid being too much of a perfectionist. You'll make life far easier for yourself – and others.
8 Laugh at life. Seeing the funny side of even serious situations helps you handle them more effectively.
9 Co-operate more often than you compete. If you stop being a threat to others they are less likely to pose any threat to you. And you'll feel less emotionally and physically tense about achieving your goals.
10 Open up to others – make the first move now and again. It will help boost your confidence.

11 Set aside time for doing things which you find entertaining and enjoyable. Don't feel guilty about taking time for yourself.
12 Love yourself. Avoid being overly harsh or self-critical. The only person you'll hurt is you.

10

FOOD FOR A HEALTHY HEART

There is no such thing as unhealthy fresh food — only unhealthy eating habits. When consumed to excess any food will do you harm. The key to a wholesome diet is moderation and balance.

We are going to explain how to enhance and safeguard the health of your heart through an informed and sensible attitude towards the food you eat. We are not suggesting specific menus, rather providing general guidelines. Within the constraints of Plan-21, our diet programme which is described in the next chapter, you can eat whatever you wish. However, implementing Plan-21 will probably mean reducing consumption of some types of foods while eating more of the foodstuffs you may be presently neglecting or eating in insufficient amounts.

Changing Lifestyles – Changing Risks

If we exclude infant mortality, the average life span of the twentieth-century human is no longer, despite the technological advances in medicine and hygiene, than it was in the nineteenth century.

A century ago the major causes of death were tuberculosis and pneumonia. With the arrival of antibiotics and improved public health these dangers declined, being replaced by today's major killers, cardiovascular disease and cancer. These diseases are, in many cases, entirely preventable. Unfortunately cultural evolution has outstripped our biological evolution.

The last 100 years have seen dramatic changes in our environment and in lifestyles, changes to which the human body has not yet been able to adapt. As a result, a great many people dig their grave with their own teeth. They overindulge in foods which send their cholesterol levels soaring and clog up their coronary arteries. Around 75 per cent of the items sold by fast food companies are high in fat. Many have more than 60 per cent of their calories in the form of fat.

Let's look at a typical convenience food meal of French fries and a burger. Those tempting, thin-cut, pre-fried then refried chips you'll be served in many fast food places can contain up to 55 per cent saturated beef fat as well as concealing other unhealthy surprises.

Their colouring, for instance, may come from soaking in dyes developed for the textile industry or being sprayed with sugar prior to frying, so increasing their calorific value without adding anything to their nutritional value (see under *Carbohydrates*, below).

With more than 20 million fast food meals being eaten in Britain alone every week it's little wonder the Western way of dining leads to the Western way of dying.

While health and life expectancy in the Third World are impaired by undernutrition, in the West we suffer the same ill-effects through overnutrition. We are overfed and under-exercised. Our typical diet is low in fibre but high in refined sugar, salt and fat.

A recent report by the Royal Society of Medicine revealed that, in the average diet, the amount of fat stands at 42 per cent (against the Royal College of Medicine's recommended maximum level of 35 per cent). This has remained unchanged throughout the 1980s.

'Unlike the USA and Europe, the incidence of coronary heart disease is not declining in the UK,' comments their report. 'And Britain has one of the worst heart disease rates in the world.'

To add insult to injury we often drink too much alcohol, which, among other harmful effects, is high in calories and raises blood triglyceride levels (see below).

Combine these unhealthy eating habits with the sedentary lifestyle followed by many, and you have the perfect recipe for an excess of calories and an increase in weight.

By changing the way we eat, both the length and quality of human life is enhanced. The republic of Georgia can boast a higher proportion of healthy, active centenarians among its population than any other place on earth. Professor Givi Abdushelishvili, formerly of the Institute of Nutrition of Soviet Georgia, who has made a special study of these vigorous old people, regards diet as the key. They are moderate eaters and the calorie values of their diets are lower than those usually recommended by doctors. They eat chiefly vegetable foods which are low in saturated fats.

Following their example will not only improve your health and longevity but may even help you feel happier and more positive about life.

The Building Blocks of Health

Let's start by looking at the basic constituents of our diet and explore some of the problems which incorrect eating creates for the cardiovascular system.

To sustain life we must take in seven essential elements – protein, carbohydrates, fats, fibre, vitamins, minerals and water.

The first three provide energy which is measured in calories. Ideally we should obtain 15–20 per cent of our total calories from proteins, 30 per cent from fat and the rest from carbohydrates. Eating too much high-fat food can make this balance virtually impossible to achieve.

By eating a large burger with a large portion of French fries, fruit pie and a regular cola, a woman obtains 60 per cent of her daily calorie needs, more than 60 per cent of her daily protein and 77 per cent of her daily fat requirement. Yet it provides only a tiny amount of vitamins A (5 per cent) and C (19 per cent), together with low levels of iron (34 per cent).

To include such foods in a health-promoting eating plan, your remaining meals would have to consist of nutrient-rich, low-fat foods which supplied you with 95 per cent Vitamin A; 81 per cent Vitamin C and 66 per cent iron yet contributed less than half the day's calories and less than a quarter of its fat.

'Fast food can be part of a balanced diet,' says Tim Lobstein, author of *Fast Food Facts*,* 'but *the more fast food you eat the harder it can be to balance it.* And you might need a calculator and dietary text book to help you.'

PROTEINS
These are made up of substances known as *amino acids* strung together to form a long chain. Amino acids are the building blocks of proteins.

---

*The London Food Commission's *Fast Food Facts* (Camden Press).

Eight are termed *essential* because, since the body cannot manufacture them, good health depends on their consumption. The main structures of the body, organs, tissues and cells are all made from protein which is essential for the processes of regeneration and repair.

There are two kinds of protein – animal and vegetable. Animal protein is known as *first class protein* because it contains all the amino acids. Vegetable protein, which lacks some of these amino acids, is termed *second class protein*. The one exception is soya beans which contain all eight essential amino acids.

This deficiency can be easily remedied, however, by combining two or three different types of vegetable protein. A good rule is to mix grains with one or two other foods from the groups of pulses, nuts and small seeds (see below).

Nutritionists are agreed that in the affluent West we eat, on average, two or three times more protein than the body needs for cell renewal. One of the consequences of this over-consumption is that larger quantities of urea must be excreted in the urine, placing a heavier workload on the kidneys.

The World Health Organization recommends a protein consumption of up to 37 grams per day for a moderately active man and 29 grams for a woman. The typical Western diet of course contains far more, many people eating their recommended daily allowance at breakfast alone.

Most of us could halve our daily intake with only beneficial effects. Over-consumption of animal protein may lead to deficiencies of vitamins B_6 and niacin, as well as calcium, iron, zinc, magnesium and phosphorus. During digestion, excess meat in the diet leads to a build-up in toxins which causes harm to the cells.

Fish can save your heart

Eskimos eat hardly any fibre, few carbohydrates, have few vitamins C or E and their diet is rich in protein. According to all we have said so far, they should be suffering appalling rates of coronary heart disease. Yet Greenland Eskimos seldom have heart disease, hypertension is rare and their blood cholesterol levels are remarkably low.

For decades this finding has presented nutritionists with a baffling paradox. Now the mystery is solved. The Eskimo diet, which includes more fish than any other race in the world, is rich in polyunsaturated fatty acids of the *Omega-3* group. This group of unsaturated fatty acids has now been shown to safeguard the heart by reducing cholesterol and triglycerides while keeping arteries clear of blood clots.

Omega-3 also protects the Japanese, whose fish consumption is six times greater than in the West, from heart disease.

The even better news is that Omega-3, which has been described as the decade's most important nutritional discovery, is obtained easily and cheaply from fish.

The highest levels are found in Norwegian sardines (5.1 grams per 100 gram serving) and lowest in haddock (0.16 grams per 100 gram serving).

But Omega-3 is not the only reason why in the diet plan described in the next chapter we advise a significant increase in fish consumption. Fish is also an excellent, low-calorie source of protein. A 100 gram (3.5 oz) portion of cooked white fish provides one-third of your daily requirements for less than 100 calories.

Fish livers are rich in vitamins A and D, the flesh in B vitamins, particularly B_6 and niacin. Fish will also provide you with potassium, iodine, selenium, iron and phosphorus. Prawns, scallops and unboned fish, like sardines, are excellent sources of calcium and contain fluoride to protect your teeth against decay.

And there is yet more benefit to be derived from eating more fish. They are one of the richest sources of nucleic acid. By increasing consumption you safeguard your DNA (deoxyribonucleic acid) and RNA (ribonucleic acid), the genetic blueprints which control every aspect of bodily function.

Very fatty fish such as herring, mackerel and sardines are high in the polyunsaturated fat eicosapentaenoic acid (EPA) from which series three prostaglandins are made. This hormone-like substance lowers blood triglycerides and cholesterol. It also stops blood platelets sticking together and thus reduces the risk of clots forming in the vessels.

CARBOHYDRATES

These are compounds of carbon, hydrogen and oxygen whose main function is to provide energy. They are divided into simple and complex types, commonly known as *sugars* and *starches*. Simple sugars can be further separated into *monosaccharides* and *disaccharides*. The monosaccharides are the basic units of all carbohydrates and link together to produce disaccharides (two units) and polysaccharides (many units), the complex carbohydrate of starch. Monosaccharides are glucose, galactose and fructose.

Sucrose, loosely termed sugar, is a disaccharide obtained from sugar cane or sugar beet. It is the most commonly consumed. It is also, due to refining, one of the most hazardous.

White and deadly

Sucrose is called a disaccharide, because during digestion it is broken down into glucose and fructose; 100 grams of sucrose gives 53 grams of glucose and 53 grams of fructose.

Food for a Healthy Heart

For most of human history we have consumed small quantities of sugar, in the form of fructose obtained from the fruits and honey. Two hundred years ago only about 8 grams of fructose were eaten daily.

Today we consume around 4 ounces (125 grams) of sucrose, equal to 66 grams of fructose, each day. When fructose obtained from fruit is added to this it brings the average total to some 75 grams daily, almost 10 times more than our digestive system has evolved to handle. The adverse consequences for our health are severe.

First, sugar offers calories without nourishment. Like those in alcohol they are 'empty calories'. This means it meets your energy requirements while starving your body of the raw materials essential for healthy growth.

When Professor John Yudkin, Emeritus Professor of Nutrition at London University, compared the rate of coronary heart disease with sugar intake across 15 countries, he discovered the death rate per 100,000 people rose steadily from 60 for each 20 pounds of sugar consumed per head, to 300 for 120 pounds and 750 for 150 pounds.

The conclusion is that the risk of heart disease could be significantly reduced by eating less sugar. Unfortunately this is easier said than done.

The hazard of hidden sugar

We eat far more sugar than we realize, mainly because it is hidden in other foods, most of which are not considered to have a high sugar content. Even if you drink tea or coffee without sugar and never sprinkle any on your breakfast cereal, the chances are you'll still be consuming more than around a quarter of a pound per day, or more than half your weight, around 100lbs, every year.

This comprises 'processed' or 'commercial' sugar, which

Professor Yudkin once described as 'pure white and deadly', a headline-catching but not entirely accurate phrase since brown sugar is just as harmful as white.

While sales of white sugar have gradually declined in recent years, as people became more health conscious, individual consumption has actually *increased* without people being any the wiser.

How can we consume so much without realizing the fact?

The answer is to be found in processed foods. Ten years ago around half the sugar eaten came out of the sugar bowl. Today a staggering 2,500,000 tons a year, or two-thirds of our annual consumption, lies concealed within other food products as the table below reveals.

Foodstuff	*Approximate sugar in grams*
Chocolate digestive biscuit	9
Shortcake biscuit	2
Slice sponge cake	7
Doughnut	11
Slice chocolate cake	9
Small chocolate bar	17
Packet instant custard	34
Small carton fruit yoghurt	22
Portion apple crumble	24
Pint of beer	13
Can Coca-Cola	35
Small tin of fruit	26

Sugar is also present in some unexpected products. Many brands of muesli, despite their healthy image, contain 25 per cent sugar. Four tablespoons at breakfast add almost 16 grams to your daily consumption. And unless the label specifically says otherwise, you can bet all tinned food contains sugar. A small can of baked beans, for example, has 10 grams while a similar sized tin of sweetcorn or kidney beans contains 7 grams. Three teaspoons of coffee essence will give you 5 grams of hidden sugar.

FATS

A hundred years ago, fat constituted less than a quarter of the average diet. Today nearly half our energy is obtained from fats in different forms.

Fats are formed by the combination of glycerol with three fatty acids. What makes the crucial difference is the type of fatty acids in the molecule.

Saturated fatty acids are those in which the molecules contain as much hydrogen as they are able to combine with. Usually solid at room temperature, they are found in many foods, including dairy products, some margarine and meat.

Monounsaturated fatty acids are those in which the fatty acid can, under the right conditions, combine with another hydrogen atom. They are normally liquid at room temperature, but will solidify if left in a cold place. They are present in virtually all food, but especially in certain vegetable oils, such as olive oil (see Chapter 11 for the beneficial effects of this oil).

Polyunsaturated fats are those capable of taking up more than one atom of hydrogen. They remain liquid at room temperature and are found in a wide range of foods, including oily fish, nuts, certain margarines and some vegetable oils, for instance sunflower and corn oil.

It is misleading to describe animal fats as saturated and vegetable fats as polyunsaturated, since all fats found in food consist of a mixture of different types of fatty acids.

However, the mixture in animal fats contains more saturated fatty acids than the mixture found in vegetable fats, while a vegetable fat mixture contains more polyunsaturated fatty acids than does animal fat. But there are important exceptions.

Some manufacturers boast their product contains only vegetable oil, clearly implying you will be consuming the safer, polyunsaturated mix of fatty acids. On reading the label's small print, however, you may discover the vegetable in question is coconut or palm oil, both of which are high in saturated fats.

Equally you should not be put off buying fish (see above) in the belief that, since it is animal, the fat will be saturated. Fish oils tend to be high in polyunsaturated fatty acids.

When one comes to margarine, the difference between animal and vegetable fats gets more complicated. To ensure that the polyunsaturated vegetable (43 per cent) or fish oil (43 per cent) fat used remains hard enough to spread at room temperature, it goes through a process known as *hydrogenation*. This changes some of the polyunsaturated fatty acids into saturated fatty acids and a group of fatty acids called *trans fats*. These are present in large amounts in hard margarine and other fats which have been artificially hardened.

In 1984 the Committee on Medical Aspects of Food Policy (COMA) advised that: 'Trans fatty acids should be regarded as equivalent to saturated fatty acids for the purposes of recommendations to the general public.' This means some types of margarine, especially those which are hard, are similar to butter in terms of their saturated fat content.

The significance for cardiovascular health is that saturated fats pose a greater risk than the polyunsaturated variety since they tend to increase levels of blood cholesterol. COMA recommend an upper limit of 15 per cent of our total energy requirement (see below) coming from saturated fats.

Fat and cholesterol

In a study of 356,222 American men aged between 35 and 57, Dr Jeremiah Stamler of Northwestern University Medical School in the USA found increased risk of heart disease began with cholesterol levels around 180 milligrams per 100 millilitres of blood, a level many doctors consider safe. Dr Stamler's research showed the relationship between levels of cholesterol and mortality was represented by a gradual curve.

With cholesterol levels between 182 and 202 the death rate, over a six-year period, among men who developed coronary heart disease was 29 per cent. Between 203 and 220 it was 73 per cent; 221–245 raised it to 121 per cent, while at higher levels still mortality risk increased by 242 per cent. This was true even for non-smokers whose blood pressure was normal.

He also found, however, that by reducing the intake of saturated fats and high cholesterol foods the risk could be considerably reduced.

Fat is not bad food

Although mistakenly viewed as the enemy of good health, fats are, in reality, vital to health. Weight for weight they provide twice as many calories as carbohydrates.

They also contain linoleic and alphalinolenic acids, known as *essential fatty acids*. These are involved in the structure of cell membranes, and serve as precursors of hormone-like substances called *prostaglandins* which are absolutely necessary for good health. Fat only becomes hazardous when eaten to excess and of the saturated variety.

How much fat should we eat?

According to a report by the UK National Advisory Committee on Nutritional Education (NACNE) our total energy consumption should be derived from food sources in these proportions:

Protein	11%
Fat	30%
Carbohydrate	55%
Alcohol	4%

The late Dr Nathan Pritikin, author of the famous Pritikin diet, recommended patients at the Longevity Center in Santa Barbara, California, to make fat no more than 10 per cent of their diet. In practice, most people find it hard to persevere with this Pritikin diet, but can manage to follow the advice of the American Heart Association which proposes a maximum of 30 per cent fat.

The table below shows approximately what different foodstuffs will contribute to your diet.

Source	Percentage of total diet
Meat products	26
Margarine	13
Cooking fats	12
Milk	12
Butter	11
Cheese and cream	7
Biscuits, cakes and pastry	6
Eggs	3
Other	10

FIBRE

Fibre is found in foods such as nuts, small seeds, pulses (peas, beans and lentils) and whole grains, fresh raw fruits and vegetables. It used to be termed *roughage* as it was generally rough in texture and passed through the body unchanged, giving bulk to the stools. However, there are two different types of fibre – *insoluble* and *soluble*.

Soluble fibre is mainly digested while insoluble fibre, such as wheat bran, passes through the gut unchanged, absorbing water as it goes.

The result is a faster passage through the gut and softer, bulkier stools. This has the beneficial result of diluting and rapidly eliminating any toxins in the digestive tract.

There are three kinds of hard, insoluble fibre: *cellulose, hemicellulose* and *lignin*.

Soft soluble fibre comes in two types, *pectin* and *gums*. Before being broken down soluble fibre forms a gel as it absorbs water from the gut. Pectin is found in fruit and vegetables, while gums are present in oats and pulses. A balanced diet will include an adequate amount of both soluble and insoluble fibre obtained from whole grains, nuts, small seeds, pulses, fruit and vegetables.

The value of fibre has long been extolled by doctors. In America Doctor Kellogg developed cornflakes for his patients, although today sugar has been added to the original recipe. Dr Bircher-Benner, inventor of muesli, found raw fruit and cereals were health-promoting.

Until quite recently fibre was regarded as a 'crank' food only eaten by eccentrics. Today its key role in healthy eating is widely recognized with new discoveries about its nutritional benefits being made all the time.

Wheat bran, long advocated for ensuring efficient digestion, was recently shown to assist in the metabolism of sugar and fat. University of Surrey researchers added wheat bran to the diets of volunteers and then examined blood cholesterol levels. After eating between 7 and 12 grams (two to three tablespoons) of unprocessed wheat bran daily for six weeks (the precise amount depended on their weight) the volunteers' high density lipid cholesterol (the beneficial variety) had risen by 46 per cent while levels of harmful low density lipid cholesterol had decreased by a quarter. The bran, sprinkled on soups and desserts, raised their dietary fibre consumption by one-third.

Fruit and vegetables

Coronary heart disease is rare among the working-class population of Naples where blood cholesterol levels are low and obesity seldom a problem. These low-paid Italians are protected by their poverty which prevents them from enjoying the high-animal-protein main courses and sugar-rich desserts popular with their wealthier countrymen. Instead they consume large quantities of fresh fruit, which, as we have seen, protects the body against a whole range of health problems, including cardiovascular disease and cancer.

A study of more than one million Japanese males, carried out over an 11-year period by the American Cancer Society, produced strong evidence that fresh fruit and fresh fruit juice offered a high degree of protection against cancer. Those eating fresh fruit six or seven times a week were least likely to develop the disease.

Because fruit is low in sodium it can safely be eaten by people with high blood pressure. A large peach, for example, contains less than 1mg of sodium while a glass of milk has 126mg. Fruit also contains potassium, a mineral which helps reduce blood pressure. Vegetarians typically have low blood pressure, even when there is a history of hypertension in their family.

The pectin in fruit safeguards the heart by removing cholesterol from the digestive system before it can be absorbed, and may also offer protection against gallstones and colon cancer by flushing bile acids from the intestines.

Fruit sugars (mainly fructose) provide energy without producing the rapid rise in blood sugar levels which occurs after eating foods rich in sucrose. Pectin has a role to play here as well, coating the intestines with a gel-like substance which slows down the uptake of glucose.

By slowing the passage of food through the digestive system, the gel also reduces the risk of overeating due to hunger pangs.

Fruit is rich in a wide range of nutrients, including folic acid, a B vitamin required for the healthy development of red blood cells; vitamins C and B_6, and magnesium.

Fruits are also a good source of potassium, which is essential for maintaining muscle contraction, heart beat and normal blood pressure. Fruits especially rich in this essential mineral are pears, peaches, bananas and oranges. As the table on page 186 shows, many vegetables, nuts and fruits are an excellent source of fibre offering high quality nourishment without a large number of calories. The following high-fibre foods should be eaten regularly:

Asparagus, mushrooms, beets, cauliflower, spinach and turnip greens supply nucleic acid, and are especially valuable for vegetarians who are unable to get theirs from fish.

Eat as much fresh fruit and vegetables as you like, although if you have a weight problem watch your consumption of bananas and avocados which are high in calories, and do not drink large quantities of concentrated fruit juice which, being high in fructose, is also rich in calories.

Seeds, which include cereals (grains), pulses, nuts and small seeds are an excellent source of protein, but as mentioned above, only supply all the essential amino acids your body needs when eaten in combination.

Food	Serving	Dietary fibre (grams)
Haricot beans (cooked)	100g	7.4
Kidney beans (cooked)	100g	7.0
Spinach (cooked)	100g	6.3
Pear (with skin)	1 large	6.2
Peas (cooked)	100g	5.2
Almonds	30g	4.2

The cereals, including wheat, oats, barley, maize, millet, rice and rye, should be eaten whole. Oats are excellent for lowering blood cholesterol because they contain soluble fibre.

Pulses provide protein and are far more beneficial than meat or sugar-rich food. If eaten in large amounts, however, they are liable to cause wind and abdominal distention so consume in moderation. They are an excellent source of gums, soluble fibre which helps reduce blood cholesterol.

Nuts, the seeds of trees, are highly nutritious. A hundred grams of almonds, for instance, will provide you with 25 per cent of your daily protein, iron, potassium and vitamin B_6 needs, and 50 per cent of your calcium, vitamin B_1 and fibre requirements, in addition to zinc and vitamin B_2.

You should avoid salted nuts for reasons given under *Salt* below. Shelled nuts should be bought in small quantities and can be kept for months in a refrigerated airtight container. Because nuts contain polyunsaturated fats, which are unstable, they rapidly oxidize and become rancid, forming substances known as *free radicals*, which can be harmful to the body cells.

Small seeds from various plants such as sunflower, sesame, alfalfa, linseed and rape are high in nutrients. Make certain you always eat them fresh. Alfalfa seeds are thought to lower blood cholesterol due to the presence of substances called *saponins*.

Whenever possible eat organically grown vegetables free from pesticide residues and make certain they are fresh. If feasible, eat your vegetables raw, preferably with their skins on. Because most of the goodness is close to the skins, peeling removes this nutritious layer. Steam rather than boil vegetables when cooking, but if boiling, use as little water as possible and bring it to the boil *before* adding the vegetables.

When shopping for fruit and vegetables look for relatively unblemished fruit. Avoid any which are obviously damaged, overripe or badly wrinkled. Much of their goodness has been lost during transportation and storage. It's best to select fruits which are starting to ripen rather than unripe ones. They should feel firm and, in many cases, have a slightly sweet smell. Buy in season whenever possible.

VITAMINS

So called because all were once believed to be substances called *amines* and were also known to be essential for life. It is now recognized not all vitamins are amines. Some, such as vitamins B and C, are water soluble, cannot be stored by the body and pass through the system. Others, for instances, A, D, E and K are fat soluble and can be stored within the body. The essential fatty acids are sometimes designated as vitamin F.

In the view of most doctors, an adequate diet will provide

all the vitamins necessary for proper health.

While it is true that eating correctly ensures you get your recommended daily allowance (RDA) of both vitamins and minerals there is good evidence that taking additional vitamins and minerals in the form of supplements can be beneficial. Accordingly this is what we advocate in our Plan-21 diet.

MINERALS

Minerals are essential for health and can be divided into *macrominerals*, which are needed in large amounts, and *trace elements* where only very small quantities are necessary for health. The macrominerals are calcium, phosphorus, sodium, potassium, chlorine and magnesium.

WATER

Water is the major constituent of the body. We are 60 per cent water, some two-thirds of which is held within the cells themselves.

The water required to sustain life comes from the fluids we drink, the foods eaten and complex metabolic processes going on within the body. We need a minimum of 1.75 litres (approximately 3 pints) a day to remain healthy. On average 1 litre comes from fluids, 400ml from food and 3,250ml from the metabolism of food. Water leaves the body in urine, faeces and by evaporation from the skin and lungs.

Unless you are suffering from kidney disease or heart failure, the more water you drink, within reason, the better. After proteins, carbohydrates and fats it is our most important nutrient.

An important function is flushing away toxins and other harmful substances removed by the blood. The more water drunk, the more urine produced and the less work the kidneys have to do since dilute urine is excreted more easily than concentrated urine.

Drinking plenty of water also helps to prevent crystals forming in the body fluids. Gout, for example, results from an accumulation of sodium urate crystals in the joints and tendons: kidney stones (urinary calculi) are typically urates of calcium and magnesium.

You can become dehydrated without being stranded in a desert. Any exertion which makes you sweat, some types of medication, and pregnancy will all significantly increase your body's water requirements. With age the brain's thirst mechanism tends to work less efficiently, which means older people may easily suffer mild dehydration without realizing it.

The symptoms of dehydration include light-headedness, muscle cramps, weariness, loss of appetite, impatience and irritability.

SALT

We consume around three heaped teaspoons, or approximately 10 grams of salt (sodium chloride) each day, despite the fact that our body requires less than one-tenth of a teaspoon (about 200 milligrams) of sodium daily for health.

In certain 'salt resistant' individuals this poses few problems. They are able to take up to 15 grams daily without, apparently, being adversely affected. But many people – perhaps half the adult population – damage their health by eating too much salt and if high blood pressure runs in your family the chances are you are among them.

There is a relationship between salt and high blood pressure, the connecting link being sodium. Body sodium is mostly found in the fluid which bathes the cells. In fact it is actively expelled from the cells by means of a mechanism called the sodium pump. Eating too much salt leads to such an excess of sodium within the cells that the pump becomes overwhelmed.

Potassium is then displaced from the cells, causing them to malfunction and resulting in increased blood pressure. While especially dangerous for hypertension sufferers, this is not much safer for people with normal blood pressure.

During the 1930s the late Dr Max Gerson, best known for his work in the treatment of cancer, developed a hypothesis that all diseases – including cancer – start due to an imbalance between sodium and potassium in the cells. Dr Gerson's answer was a diet low in sodium and high in potassium, low in fat but high in vitamins, minerals and fluids. This he achieved by using fresh, organically grown vegetables and fruit, both eaten raw and in the form of juices.

Reducing salt intake is especially important if you suffer from hypertension. But we can all benefit greatly by drastically limiting our consumption. The table below shows where most people get their salt.

Foodstuff	Percentage
Added at the table or in cooking	33
Cereals and bread	33
Meat and meat products	17
Other foods	17

ALCOHOL

Many people obtain a high proportion of calories from alcoholic drinks. Unfortunately, as with the calories obtained from sucrose, these provide the body with no nourishment and are, therefore, termed 'empty calories'. This increases the risk of obesity as well as raising levels of triglycerides in the blood. As we have seen this is a risk factor in coronary heart disease.

Research by the British Heart Foundation refutes the widely held belief that a little alcohol offers a protection against heart attacks. A long-term study involving 7,735 men in 24 towns did suggest that moderate drinkers had an even lower rate of heart disease than teetotallers. However, this group also included the lowest proportion of manual workers and the lowest percentage of smokers. They also had lower than average blood pressure and fewer of them were overweight.

Gerald Shaper, Professor of Clinical Epidemiology at the Royal Free Hospital medical school commented:

> *It seems very likely that the apparent protection from heart attacks in regular light drinkers is due to these multiple advantages experienced over a lifetime, rather than any direct effect of alcohol.*

Even if it does not do you any good, alcohol taken in moderation will not cause any great harm either. But the emphasis is on *moderation*.

TEA AND COFFEE
Again, when drunk in moderation, up to, say, four cups per day, these should pose no threat to health. But consume much more and you could suffer a variety of harmful consequences.

Caffeine, which is also found in cocoa, chocolate and cola, is a powerful stimulant affecting the heart and its arteries as well as kidneys, lungs, brain and central nervous system. It is thought to inhibit an enzyme used to break down the energy-producing substance cyclic adenosine monophosphate (AMP). This rise in cyclic AMP stimulates glucose production so making more energy available to the cells whose activity increases.

The caffeine content of different beverages and food is shown in the table below.

Doses as low as 100mg increase levels of mental and physical arousal. The brain becomes more wakeful and alert, the heart pumps blood faster, coronary arteries dilate, improving the heart's own blood supply. By contrast, blood vessels of the brain constrict, reducing blood flow and bringing relief from headaches due to hypertension.

	Caffeine (mg per cup)
Coffee:	
percolated	110–165
instant	90–135
decaffeinated	2–5
Tea (Indian) brewed for:	
one minute	10–35
three minutes	20–40
five minutes	25–60
Cocoa	3–10
Chocolate (1 oz):	
milk	1–15
cooking	25–30
Cola (per bottle)	35–45

When drunk in moderation, therefore, caffeine has pleasant psychological and physiological effects. In excess, however, it leads to insomnia, restlessness, anxiety and depression. Your heart may start beating irregularly and, at high doses, caffeine poisoning may produce mild delirium.

In common with all stimulants, a rebound effect is experienced as the drug wears off, energy gives way to lethargy, and enthusiasm to gloom. Alertness is replaced by fatigue and a significant decline in performance.

Dr Annette Rossignol of Tufts University, Massachusetts, found a connection between caffeine and premenstrual tension. Sixty-one per cent of women drinking 4.5 to 15 caffeine-rich drinks a day reported moderate to severe symptoms, compared with only 16 per cent of non-caffeine drinkers.

WHAT'S WRONG WITH OUR DIET?

It has long been assumed that a diet high in protein, especially animal protein, and low in carbohydrates is most beneficial to health. A typical day's menu might include a fry-up of eggs, bacon and sausages for breakfast, meat with two vegetables for lunch and a further meat meal to end the day. Unfortunately, these foods are not only high in protein, but also fat – even lean cuts of red meat always contain a substantial proportion of saturated fats.

Carbohydrates were shunned because they were regarded as fattening and believed to contribute little of real value by way of essential nutrients.

The humble potato was virtually banned from the dinner table. All these assumptions are wrong, and in the next chapter we will explain how they can be corrected by following our easily implemented Plan-21 diet suggestions.

11

PLAN-21 — YOUR KEY TO A HEALTHY HEART
III Action Chapter III

This 21-point diet plan includes *seven* foods to eat in greater quantities; *seven* foods whose intake should be reduced and *seven* general changes you may need to make to your eating habits. Starting from today you should:

Increase your consumption of:
- Fresh fruit
- Raw vegetables
- Fish
- Fibre
- Organically grown foods
- Different foods in your diet
- Water

Decrease your consumption of:
- Refined carbohydrate
- Salt
- Saturated fats
- Cholesterol
- Tea and coffee
- Alcohol
- Calories

At the same time:
- Eat smaller amounts – chew properly
- Avoid distractions while eating
- Break bad eating habits
- Take care over cooking
- Take additional fat-soluble vitamins
- Take additional water-soluble vitamins
- Take additional minerals

When followed diligently, Plan-21 will safeguard your cardiovascular system, improve your health and help you enjoy a long and vigorous life.

Putting It Into Practice

INCREASE – FRUIT AND VEGETABLES

Ensure that at least one meal a day includes a substantial quantity of raw vegetables, chopped or grated. Eat fruit for dessert and for snacks between meals. Apples, oranges, grapes and berries are good sources of pectin and should be eaten regularly. If possible make most or all of the following seven fruits and vegetables a part of your weekly diet.

1 Cantaloupe melons

Half a cantaloupe at breakfast provides more than one day's basic dietary requirements of vitamins A and C, as well as significant amounts of calcium and iron. Despite providing only 60 calories, the fruit's bulk means it satisfies your appetite and cuts down the desire for high calorie snacks such as chocolate.

2 Beans

As previously stated, soyabeans contain all the essential

amino acids found in meat protein. Other beans are lacking in only two. They are richer in calcium and phosphorus than meat and supply both iron and B vitamins. On the other hand they have half the calories of meat and none of the fat.

3 Kale
This dark, leafy, cabbage-like vegetable is low in calories (30 per cupful) yet loaded with vitamins and minerals. For example, one cupful provides 8,140 International Units of vitamin A, nearly twice the recommended daily allowance. It will also provide up to one-quarter of your daily iron requirement, is a rich source of calcium and contains a host of vital micronutrients such as copper and iodine.

4 Avocado
Contains large amounts of nine vitamins, including B complex and C. It also supplies your body with calcium, phosphorus and iron, together with trace elements of 11 additional minerals.

The avocado also contains around 25 grams of polyunsaturated fat but no cholesterol. In a study Dr Wilson Grant of the American Veterans Administration fed an avocado a day to 16 men with high blood pressure. Some weeks later when the study came to an end, half the men had significantly lower levels of cholesterol. But remember that an avocado provides around 370 calories, so eat in moderation especially if — as mentioned above — you have a weight problem.

5 Apples
When a group of healthy French subjects were given an apple a day, 80 per cent had a significant reduction in blood cholesterol, while researchers at Yale found even the smell of

apples could lower blood pressure. Apples are also a fair source of potassium (100 grams will supply approximately 5 per cent of your daily requirement) and fibre.

6 Grapefruit

Has been found to lower blood cholesterol and so protect the arteries. Eat as much of the white part of the fruit as possible. When buying select those which feel smoothest and densest. The riper they are, the greater their vitamin C content. Pink grapefruits have higher levels of vitamin A.

7 Olive oil

A mainly monounsaturated fat (75 per cent of olive oil is of this type), it has been credited with the low rate of heart disease found among people living around the Mediterranean. This was confirmed by Italian doctors using young volunteers who ate either a standard low-fat diet or Italian-style food of salad, vegetables, bread and pasta enriched with olive oil. Their results, recently published in the *American Journal of Clinical Nutrition*, showed that amounts of the damaging LDL cholesterol, the low density variety which clogs arteries, were reduced more in those eating olive oil than the ones eating a standard low-fat diet. Beneficial HDL cholesterol remained unchanged in both groups.

Use olive oil to replace some of the other saturated fats left in your diet (see list overleaf). Olive oil is safer to cook with than a polyunsaturated oil, since it will not oxidize to produce harmful substances called free radicals when heated. One tablespoon of olive oil provides around 10 grams of monounsaturated fat. You can obtain the same quantity from the following:

Canola oil	
(a flavour-free oil made from rapeseed)	4 teaspoons
Peanuts	¼ cup
Avocado	half
Hazelnuts	3 tablespoons
Peanut butter	3 tablespoons

But remember that olive oil is very fattening and should only be consumed in moderation.

INCREASE – FISH

Eat fish a minimum of four days a week and sardines at least twice a week. They provide the most Omega-3 and nucleic acids. Excellent sources of both are salmon (3g Omega-3 per 100g serving); mackerel (2.18g Omega-3 per 100g serving) and herring (1.09g Omega-3 per serving). Fish with a low Omega-3 rating include haddock, flounder and bass. Avoid kippers whose (nutritionally unnecessary) colouring is produced by a substance called Brown FX. Research suggests the possibility of adverse health effects from two of this mixture of synthetic azo dye's constituents.

Sadly, most shallow coastal water is now so polluted by heavy metals from industrial wastes, it is wiser to eat fish trawled in deep waters, farmed commercially or from clean mountain streams.

Shellfish taken out of polluted waters may contain toxins, in addition to organisms responsible for hepatitis, cholera and gastro-enteritis.

Always but your fish as fresh as possible, and keep chilled to guard against bacteria. Eat as soon as possible after purchase.

INCREASE – FIBRE

We have already described ways of increasing the fibre in your diet by eating more fruit and vegetables. In addition, change from processed cereals to whole or lightly milled grain. Make brown rice, rye, maize flours and rolled oats a regular part of your diet. Add bran, from one to three tablespoons depending on your weight, to your food eat day. When choosing a cereal, read the label carefully. As a general rule, the shorter the list of contents the more nutritional the product.

Whole grains should be first on the list and you should avoid any which are laden with fat or refined sugar. These can make up to 60 per cent of the weight in some popular breakfast foods.

In the average serving of cereal (around 30 grams) this amounts to four teaspoons. Ensure your calories, which vary from 50 to 130, come from eating the complex carbohydrates in grains rather than those in simple sugars.

The ratio of total carbohydrates to protein ought to be about 8:1. Where it is greater there is probably too much refined sugar present. Check the fat content too, as some brands of cereals contain as much fat per serving as in two pats of butter. Beware of coconut or palm oils (see above) since these are saturated fats.

INCREASE – ORGANICALLY GROWN FOODS

While buying this type of food is usually more expensive and often more inconvenient, it is well worth the extra expenditure and effort. After all, having good health should be a number one priority. The nutritional value of food starts to decline from the moment it has been gathered. Some supermarket oranges, for example, have been found to have little or no vitamin C. It had all disappeared during the time taken to get it from the orchards to the stores. Apart from – usually – being fresher, organically grown food is less likely to be contaminated with pesticides, herbicides or lead.

INCREASE – VARIETY IN YOUR DIET
Food intolerance is far more common than is generally realized. Many of the sufferers are not even aware they have a problem and attribute their irritability, fatigue or depression to stress, the time of year or the weather rather than the real culprit, the food they eat. Reduce your risk of an unrecognized intolerance problem by eating a wide variety of foods.

INCREASE – WATER CONSUMPTION
Consume at least two litres (four pints) of water every day. But avoid drinking before, during or immediately after meals to prevent diluting the gastric juices and impairing digestion. When flying on a journey lasting more than one hour, drink a pint an hour. This is advisable because the jet's air conditioning system causes rapid dehydration. This, as much as crossing time zones, is responsible for the jet-lag suffered by air travellers.

Now for the seven things to *decrease* in your diet.

DECREASE – REFINED CARBOHYDRATES
If you take sugar with tea or coffee, substitute a sweetener. One heaped teaspoon of sugar contains around 9 grams of sucrose.

Eat breakfast cereals without adding sugar, as even a light sprinkling may contain around 30 grams.

Rather than pastries, sweets or other desserts with a high sugar content, eat fresh fruit. Drink no more than three soft drinks per week and preferably cut them out entirely.

Check the contents of canned foods for ingredients like 'sucrose', 'dextrose', 'maltose', 'raw sugar', 'demerara sugar', 'glucose syrup' and 'molasses'; they are all empty calorie sugars.

We do not have a naturally sweet tooth. Our apparently insatiable appetite for sweet things is merely a bad habit developed during childhood. With a little persistence you can retrain your taste buds not to desire high levels of sweetness.

Reduce your present consumption of sugar by just 50 per cent and the risk of coronary heart disease is cut by a factor of 15. In addition the danger of contracting adult onset diabetes is significantly reduced.

DECREASE – SALT
Eat less cheese; tinned vegetables; pot noodles; crisps; biscuits; salted nuts; bacon; ham; salami; sausages; fish fingers; burgers; stock cubes; smoked and tinned fish; meat and yeast extracts; packet soups. They all have a high salt content. Also check the labels on breakfast cereals since many are high in sodium.

Foods with less than 200mg of sodium per 100g include: herbs, spices, garlic, vinegar, lemon juice, fresh and frozen vegetables, unsalted nuts, raisins and raw fruit, margarine. Breakfast cereals with low sodium content are oats, muesli, Puffed Wheat and Shredded Wheat. Reduce your consumption of processed food and eat more foods high in potassium (see *Fruit* on p.197).

DECREASE – SATURATED FATS – CHOLESTEROL
Try to have several meatless days each week and try to eat in proportion to the amount of physical energy you use up each day. Choose fowl or game in preference to red meat. But if you do eat red meat, always select the leanest cuts.

All dairy products, which includes milk, eggs, butter and cheese, are high in saturated fat. But since they are also high in first class protein, vitamins and minerals, this does not mean you must exclude them from your diet entirely. Only avoid them in their high fat state. Use skimmed milk in place of full cream milk. Rather than cream put a low-fat yoghurt on your desserts.

Genuine yoghurt is a wonderfully healthy food because it contains a large amount of a friendly bacteria, *Lactobacillus acidophilus*, which takes up residence in the gut and aids digestion. When you are given antibiotics this bacteria is destroyed along with the harmful ones, leading to poor digestion.

Choose low-fat cheeses, such as cottage cheese; replace butter with a brand of margarine low in saturated fats and consume it only in very small quantities. Eat no more than two eggs per week and, if your blood cholesterol level is high, avoid them completely.

DECREASE – TEA AND COFFEE
Reduce your caffeine intake slowly, especially if you currently drink more than eight cups a day. Experiment with different substitutes, such as herb teas and decaffeinated coffee.

DECREASE – ALCOHOL
Alcohol is measured in units, with a standard single of spirits, half a pint of beer or a glass of wine counting as one unit. Ideally, cut out alcohol entirely. If this is not possible, reduce your consumption to no more than two units a day.

At between three and seven units a day harmful effects will begin, while prolonged consumption above eight units will cause progressive and steady damage to brain and liver, although these effects may not become apparent for several years.

DECREASE – CALORIES

On average a man needs between 2,000 and 3,500 kilocalories a day, while a woman requires from 1,600 to 2,400 kilocalories. The precise amount depends on how much work is being done and the surrounding temperature. On cold days the body must burn up more food energy in order to maintain its core temperature at 37°C/98.4°F.

The energy value of foods is determined by burning them in a sealed container and measuring the amount of heat produced. Per 100 grams different foods yield the following results:

	Kilocalories
Fat	900
Starch	415
Protein	430
Sucrose, lactose (milk sugar), maltose	395
Glucose and fructose	375

Where do most of us obtain these calories? A survey of 12,000 US adults revealed the most important sources of this food energy to be:

White bread, rolls and crackers	9.6%
Doughnuts, cookies and cake	5.7%
Alcohol	5.6%
Milk	4.7%
Hamburgers, cheeseburgers and meatloaf	4.4%

A similar pattern is found throughout Europe.

The average Westerner obtains nearly half (46 per cent) of their calories from carbohydrate (starch 20 per cent, sucrose 20 per cent, naturally occurring sugars 6 per cent); 42 per cent from fats and 12 per cent from protein.

As we have explained, for health this pattern of eating should be changed so that fat is reduced to 30 per cent and protein to 10 per cent of the total, while the consumption of carbohydrates is increased until it provides the remainder of our energy needs. Within this 60 per cent, starch ought to supply 30 per cent while sucrose and naturally occurring sugars each provide 10 per cent.

Another important point to bear in mind is that all calories are not created equal. It used to be believed that a calorie was a calorie no matter what food type it came from. But this conventional wisdom has been disproved by studies at Stanford University and the Human Nutrition Research Center in Beltsville, Maryland.

In one research project one group of overweight women were given a high-fat diet while another group received a lower-fat diet. Both provided the same total of calories. It was found that women on a diet where fat provided 40 per cent of their calories gained weight more easily than did those on the lower-fat diet.

A similar project, this time using obese males, came to the same conclusion. A likely explanation is the ease with which the body can convert food fat to body fat. But 23 per cent of calories are used up converting carbohydrates or protein to body fat. The simple message for watching one's weight is that fat is more fattening. 'No longer is it sufficient just to count the calories,' says Dr Kelly D. Brownell of the University of Pennsylvania School of Medicine. 'People need to pay attention to where those calories come from.'

An occasional indulgence in fast food is not going to cause much harm, provided you try to balance out the high levels of fat present in many such meals. But in general the best advice is to junk the junk. Avoid the temptation to indulge in these nutritionally unsound and unhealthy foods.

Finally we come to the seven changes which you should make in your eating habits.

1 – EAT SMALLER AMOUNTS AT EACH MEAL

Avoid swamping your system. When your digestion is forced to deal with large quantities of food, many important nutrients may not be adequately absorbed.

Ideally, instead of sitting down to three set meals a day it is healthier to 'graze' as hunger rather than habit or the clock moves you.

If this is impossible try and cut down the amount eaten at meal. By chewing your food more slowly, better digestion is ensured and you are less likely to overeat. Because we judge the amount consumed with our eyes as much as our stomachs, it often helps to place the smaller portions on smaller plates. This fools the brain into believing you are actually eating about the same quantity as before.

It is also important to take small mouthfuls and chew your food properly before swallowing. The first, essential, stage of digestion occurs in the mouth as food is broken down by the teeth and mixed with saliva, which contains the powerful enzyme ptyalin, to produce a paste that can be efficiently processed by the digestive system. Your stomach has no teeth!

Make sure your own teeth, whether natural or false, are in good shape. Regular dental check-ups are essential. An improperly masticated high-fibre diet can result in a bad case of wind.

Be the last rather than the first to finish eating and never put another forkful of food into your mouth until you have finished chewing the previous one.

2 – AVOID DISTRACTIONS WHILE EATING

Eating while watching TV or reading a newspaper is unhealthy for two main reasons. First, because it leads to the problems of poorly chewed food mentioned above, and secondly being distracted makes it easier to unintentionally overeat. By the time your brain attends to 'full' messages from the stomach you may have consumed more than is necessary.

Try and take your main meal of the day at the table so that you can sit up properly, rather than slumping in an easy chair, and hold your body in a posture which allows the digestive system to work most efficiently.

3 – BREAK BAD EATING HABITS

Many people miss breakfast completely or eat only high-carbohydrate foods, like cereals with sugar and toast.

As we have already explained, this leads to a surge of insulin and produces mid-morning energy sag as blood glucose levels fall to a point where fatigue sets in.

Busy people often skimp lunch, taking their main meal last thing at night. As a result they go to sleep on a full stomach and store rather than burn off their energy. In the morning they have no appetite for further food and the pattern of unhealthy eating is repeated.

The advice to breakfast like a king, lunch like a prince and sup like a pauper is nutritionally sound.

Eating a small meal last thing ensures you sleep more restfully and awaken with a good appetite. Protein for breakfast also assists in maintaining body weight since studies have demonstrated that, due to the body clock, calories consumed in the morning are more likely to be converted into energy than laid down as fat.

Snack on fruit, raw vegetables or whole-grain bread instead of high sugar cakes, pastries and chocolate bars.

4 – COOKING

Use stainless steel, iron or enamelled cooking utensils and prepare your food immediately prior to cooking. Leaving vegetables to soak leaches out the vitamins. Leaving the cut surfaces exposed to the air results in oxidation and destruction of vitamins. Eat foods raw whenever possible. It's surprising how many types of vegetables are enjoyable to eat raw if cut into small pieces. A hand grater is an essential kitchen utensil.

Use a marble rather than wooden chopping board, since the latter is almost impossible to clean properly and will harbour bacteria. Never allow animals into your kitchen. Salmonella is just one of the health hazards cats can bring into the food preparation area.

5 – TAKE FAT-SOLUBLE VITAMINS CORRECTLY

We suggest you take the following fat-soluble vitamins as supplements to your daily diet:

Vitamin A (Retinol):   10,000 International Units
Vitamin D (Calciferol):   400 International Units
Vitamin E (Tocopherol):   500 International Units

Be very careful not to exceed these recommended doses, however, since fat-soluble vitamins can accumulate in the body.

These vitamins are less efficiently absorbed if taken on an empty stomach or with a high-carbohydrate/low-fat meal. They require the presence of fat in the digestive system in order to reach the body. Have them with a glass of low-fat milk or following your main meal of the day.

6 – TAKE WATER-SOLUBLE VITAMINS CORRECTLY

We suggest 1 gram of powdered vitamin C (ascorbic acid) taken diluted in a little fruit juice each day. In addition, take one B-complex tablet together with a multivitamin. This helps maintain a correct balance.

These vitamins are best taken after a meal as eating aids absorption by increasing blood flow to the digestive system, so distributing all nutrients around the body more efficiently. Food also helps prevent any minor side-effects from the vitamin C, such as looseness of the bowels, caused by acidity.

7 – TAKE EXTRA CALCIUM

Take 800mg of calcium per day. As this mineral requires the presence of vitamin D and an acid environment for effective absorption, take it with a meal and, preferably, last thing at night.

Your body can obtain sufficient calcium from its food during the day, but at night may draw on natural stores – which means your skeleton – to fulfil its requirements. A calcium supplement taken immediately before bed maintains blood levels throughout the night and safeguards your bones.

If you don't eat at night then take the supplement with low-fat milk.

Using Plan-21

When following this plan be patient with yourself and don't feel guilty about occasional lapses. The only way to ensure lasting health is to make permanent changes in harmful eating habits and most people find this easier to do slowly. We suggest you introduce them a few at a time, either adding to or reducing your daily consumption of target foods over a period of weeks.

12

EXERCISE FOR A HEALTHY HEART
III Action Chapter III

For many people exercise conjures up discouraging images of exhausted marathon runners staggering across the finishing line or sweating joggers slogging wearily along feet-bruising pavements. To make matters worse, for many their first experience of exercise was compulsory PE in school, lessons which, studies show, rank second only to maths as the most detested lesson on the timetable.

The unfortunate, but unsurprising, consequence is that exercise has a bad name. Many people cannot wait to abandon all but the least demanding physical activity and sink thankfully into the lifestyle of a couch potato!

The table overleaf, derived from a 1985 study of Welsh adults, paints a picture which holds generally for both Europe and the USA.

Age	Percentage sedentary or minimally active at work or play	
	Males	Females
12–17	13.5	27.0
18–24	17.0	54.5
25–34	25.0	67.0
35–44	32.5	72.5
45–54	41.5	81.0
55–64	57.0	86.0
Total 12–64	32.0	66.5

As might be expected, younger people are more active than older ones, but by the mid-fifties over half the males and more than three-quarters of all women take virtually no exercise at all.

There is, however, evidence that this is changing. Some three million women now participate in aerobics classes; city gyms for business executives flourish; squash courts and sports halls are heavily booked and almost every modern hotel boasts a gymnasium.

While such increased interest in exercise is to be welcomed, it is not always the healthy trend one might imagine.

The trouble is that the highly competitive Type Hs who, as we have seen, are at greatest risk of coronary heart disease, often throw themselves into fitness training with the same high-pressure zeal that characterizes every other aspect of their lives.

Instead of regarding exercise as the means to an end it becomes an end in itself. Lifting weights, playing squash, jogging or running are seen as another opportunity to compete, to excel and to prove oneself a winner. A frequent result is excessive exercise inflicted on a body ill-equipped to take such punishment.

By pushing themselves beyond their physical limits at play as well as in work, unhealthy males trigger the very attack their quest for fitness was intended to prevent.

Exercise is essential to a healthy heart, but so is moderation. And that applies whether you are coming back after a heart attack or seeking to reduce the risk of CHD in the first place.

When mishandled, exercise can actually harm your health. When tackled sensibly every step taken becomes a step toward a healthier heart and a longer life.

The Value of Regular Exercise

More than two decades ago Professor David Snowdon of Loma Linda University, California, divided 3,933 healthy males aged between 30 and 63 into two groups according to the amount of exercise they took. A careful check on their health records over the next 20 years showed that those who took little exercise were nearly three times more likely to die from heart disease than active males. An interesting link was also found between inactivity and red meat consumption. Eating large amounts of red meat *and* taking little exercise more than doubled the risk of heart disease.

Similarly, a study of 12,000 heart risk patients, by researchers from the University of Minnesota School of Public Health, showed that even moderate activity reduced deaths from heart attack by up to a third, compared with sedentary males.

This decreased risk was especially associated with light to moderate activities, such as bicycling, swimming, dancing and walking. And the amount of time which needed to be invested to bring about these improvements in health could be as little as 30 minutes per day.

As the scientists commented in the *Journal of the American Medical Association*, 'This is a most encouraging finding . . . since most people should be able to schedule this amount of time for physical activity as part of their daily routine.'

Regular exercise reduces systolic blood pressure, by up to 20 points, lowers resting heart rate and improves both the cardiovascular and lymphatic systems. This ensures maximum efficiency in transporting oxygen and nutrients to the cells, and removing toxic waste products from the system.

Which Exercise Works Best?

To be effective the chosen exercise must be sufficiently intense to turn on the sympathetic (speed up) branch of the ANS. Very mild exercise will not do this, since an increase in pulse rate to at least 100 beats per minute is necessary before any training effect is achieved. The method for calculating the correct heart rate, taking into account your age and level of fitness, while exercising is explained below.

You need not jog or run to improve your health. All that's necessary is to go for a walk. It may sound too simple and undramatic to be true. But research confirms the heart-protecting value of this age-old leisure pursuit. In just a few hours each week you can walk your way to health.

WHY WALKING WINS
Going for regular walks offers many bonuses in addition to a healthy heart. Walking is:

- *Companionable.* Unlike jogging or running you never feel breathless, which means you can talk as you walk, stimulating both brain and body simultaneously.
- *Interesting.* You can visit unfamiliar places, exploring and observing your surroundings in a way which would be impossible using any other means of transport. Each bend in the road, the brow of every hill, can provide fresh vistas, exciting views and new surprises.
- *Easy and economical.* No need for expensive clothes, and you can enjoy it in towns and cities just as well as in the countryside.
- *Non-competitive.* You have neither the need nor the desire to walk faster than the next person. The temptation to drive yourself beyond your physical limits is therefore removed.
- *Rewarding.* Walking is a pleasure in itself. It is something you can look forward to and enjoy, rather than a disagreeable duty to be dreaded, delayed and dropped entirely after a few weeks.

Cardiologist Dr Henry Solomon, who considers walking the ideal exercise in virtually every respect, says that, like swimming, it 'uses the correct large muscles for conditioning; and if you swing your arms freely and naturally, you get additional benefits that way. Your pace is obviously easily varied, and you can adjust it instantly.'

THE BENEFITS OF WALKING

Research by David Mymin at the University of Manitoba in Canada showed that all the beneficial effects produced by taking strenuous exercise can be achieved equally well by simply taking a brisk walk. A study at the University of Wisconsin showed that brisk walking raised heart rate by up to 87 per cent of capacity, the same increase found in cyclists and only slightly less than that achieved by runners.

Walking has also been shown to reduce anxiety and have a beneficial effect on depression, probably by stimulating the production of endorphins. One advocate for walking as a way of enhancing mood was the philosopher and mathematician Bertrand Russell.

'Unhappy businessmen, I am convinced, would increase their happiness more by walking six miles every day than by any conceivable change in philosophy,' he commented.

If you have a stressful, intellectually demanding job then try walking as a way of making your brain work better. For centuries great writers and thinkers have been convinced that walking stimulates creativity, assists problem-solving and improves concentration. Aristotle, the Greek philosopher, was so certain that walking and thinking should go together he established the Peripatetic (walking) School of Philosophy.

French novelist Gustave Flaubert, author of *Madame Bovary*, among many classics, always took long walks before sitting down to write, claiming the exercise sharpened his imagination. Other great minds who found their mental prowess aided by long walks include William Wordsworth, who covered more than 180,000 miles in a lifetime of dedicated walking; Jane Austen, Walt Whitman, Robert Frost, Thomas Jefferson, Robert Louis Stevenson and Ralph Waldo Emerson.

AN EASY, EFFECTIVE WALKING PROGRAMME

There are seven points to remember when you start walking your way to health.

1 Avoid exercising at the start or end of the day. First thing in the morning your level of arousal is low which makes it harder to achieve the level of intensity necessary for

maximum fitness. At the end of the day fatigue creates the same problem, while vigorous exercise last thing at night can lead to disturbed sleep. The best time is around midday or early afternoon, but not within two hours of a meal.

As with any exercise it is advisable to warm up before starting out with some simple stretching routines. At the end of your walk cool down slowly rather than coming to an abrupt halt by slumping into a chair. Warming your muscles will safeguard them against being pulled while a cooling-down period prevents the blood from pooling in the extremities, causing you to feel faint. There is evidence of a sudden surge in adrenaline following vigorous exercise as your body seeks to return blood pressure to the level attained at the peak of activity. Winding down slowly prevents this and holds blood pressure steady.

Walk on grass whenever possible: it's kinder to the legs and feet.

2 Dress sensibly. A loose tracksuit with an absorbent inner surface and good quality running shoes are advisable, provided the ground is dry, even though you intend to walk rather than jog. The thick, spongy soles on properly designed running shoes absorb shocks, protecting your joints and spine. Their built-up instep avoids eversion strains on the ankle joints. Wear a thick pair of socks with a towelled inner surface to absorb sweat and prevent the foot slipping in the shoe. On long walks turn your sock inside out to avoid chafing the little toe against the seam. Take good care of your feet and keep your toenails cut short.

3 Start slowly and stop if you experience any pains in the chest; fatigue; breathlessness; faintness; dizziness; irregular

pulse or a pulse in excess of the ideal rate (see below). But don't worry that you'll come apart at the seams by embarking on a programme of sensible exercise following a heart attack.

Over a period of weeks build to the point where you walk for between 30 and 40 minutes a day. Longer if you like, and have the time, but no shorter.

4 Increase speed gradually. Although, as we explained above, health benefits are only achieved after the exercise has become sufficiently intense to switch on the sympathetic branch of the ANS, much gentler activity is desirable when you first start exercising.

Your first objective must be to build confidence and so ensure an early return to normal lifestyle. Do not proceed to more strenuous exercise without consulting your doctor.

Experiment with different strides to find one with which you feel comfortable. As you become fitter, start walking fast enough to raise your pulse to the ideal exercise rate. This is calculated by subtracting your age from 200, to obtain maximum heart rate, and then subtract a further 40 points to take into account your lack of fitness.

A 40-year-old, for instance, should walk sufficiently briskly to increase his pulse to 120 beats per minute (200 − 40 = 160; 160 − 40 = 120).

Take your pulse regularly while exercising so that you do not exceed the target rate. The best place to feel your pulse is at the side of the larynx where you can pick up the pulsation of the carotid artery. Take your pulse for six seconds then multiply by 10 to calculate the number of beats per minute. With regular exercise you'll find you must work harder to achieve your target heart rate.

The fitter you are, the slower the resting pulse and the

less time your pulse will need to return to its resting rate following exercise. After a while you need not take your pulse so often but can rely on more subjective sensations to remain at the target level. If you are taking beta-blockers, your pulse will be an unreliable guide to progress and you must rely on subjective symptoms such as fatigue and breathlessness. Never push yourself too hard. Listen to your body and rely on its wisdom.

As fitness improves you will have to exercise more intensely to achieve the same pulse rate. This could involve jogging or any of the other isotonic exercises suggested below. But do not go onto these more demanding forms of exercise until your heart, via the pulse rate, lets you know it is ready for the additional effort.

5 Watch posture. Try snapping a match with a downward pressure while holding it upright on a hard surface.

In this situation the fragile piece of wood has remarkable strength. But angle the match even slightly and try again. You'll find it splinters easily. The same law applies to the spine's 24 separate vertebrae. With the back straight and the spine upright these vertebrae are as strong as any single bone in the body.

But curve your spine and a force which was easily resisted before can cause severe damage to discs between the vertebrae which serve as shock absorbers. When extreme, this produces intense pain through pressure on the nerve fibres passing through the spinal cord to the brain.

As you walk, adopt the following posture:

- Walk tall while remaining relaxed.
- Drop your shoulders, without allowing them to fall forward.

- Hold your chin parallel with the ground. Imagine a string tending from both ears holds your head upright. Picture these strings pulled upwards, steadily and evenly, until your head feels almost weightless. Avoid tilting it back since this places unnecessary strain on neck and shoulder muscles, resulting in stiffness.

Practise walking with this posture until it feels natural and free from tension. Make all your movements comfortable, flowing and natural.

6 Try to leave your worries behind you. Observe your surroundings and forget about problems or decisions. Even when banished from the forefront of the mind, your brain continues to work on everyday tasks. Returning home from a walk you may be astonished immediately to come up with a previously elusive answer.

7 Walk whenever you are able. Climb stairs rather than use the lift. But for the first few days after returning from hospital, use the stairs only last thing at night and first thing in the morning. Never take a car when you could take a walk.

OTHER WAYS OF EXERCISING

You can enhance your health by enjoying any sort of isotonic exercises. These are activities in which the muscles are allowed to contract and there is free movement involving large muscle groups. The three goals of exercise are to increase stamina, improve suppleness and build strength. So far as good health is concerned the first two are the most important.

Isometric exercising, such as weight-lifting to increase muscle strength, prevents the muscles from shortening, so impeding the blood flow.

This forces the muscles to obtain their energy anaerobically, that is, without using oxygen. This is extremely dangerous for anybody who has had a heart attack or suffers from high blood pressure. However, the use of light weights, which allow the joints to go through their full range of movements, can be an aid to cardiopulmonary fitness.

Swimming is an excellent isotonic activity. It exercises all the major muscle groups and, because the body is supported by the water, avoids the constant shock and jarring which occur when running on hard surfaces.

Cycling, too, provides good cardiovascular exercise as well as being an interesting and rewarding activity.

One excellent form of indoor exercise which does, however, require some special equipment, is bouncing on a small trampoline. This not only stimulates the heart, but also improves lymphatic drainage since, for a brief moment at the climax of a bounce, the body defies gravity. Anxiety is reduced and depression lifted by regular 12-minute bouncing sessions.

The secret of successful exercising is *enjoyment*. Because you cannot store health or fitness, like power, in a battery, in order to be effective any exercise programme must last a lifetime, not merely a few days or weeks. If you enjoy exercising, then clearly the motivation to continue on a regular basis will be far stronger.

Seven Rules to Safeguard your Heart

1 Become aware of your hostile, cynical or aggressive thoughts. Use the stress diary to identify situations most likely to trigger such feelings. Look for common themes. Often even trivial events arouse great hostility. Challenge those thoughts and change them.

2 Talk to your partner or friends about problems and difficulties. Confession is good for the heart as well as the soul. Don't try to be – or appear – too perfect. Ask for support in your efforts to make changes. Become more trusting in relationships.
3 Put yourself in another person's position. See events from their point of view. As you do so your anger will slip away. Hostility and empathy cannot co-exist.
4 Challenge hostile thoughts with reason. As they enter your mind start an inner dialogue along these lines: 'Here I go again, working myself up. What does it matter? Why risk my heart over such a trifle?'
5 Defuse hostility with humour. But direct your laughter at the right target – yourself. Doing that is healthy. Laughing at others is simply displaying hostility through ridicule, and therefore harmful to your heart.
6 Stop angry thoughts by silently, but forcefully, ordering yourself to stop whenever they arise. This not only silences hostile ideas but prevents the anger those thoughts would otherwise generate.
7 Learn and use relaxation. It's a life-saver.

These rules have not included any mention of diet and exercise. Not because taking regular exercise or eating sensibly are unimportant, but because they have often assumed too much significance in programmes designed to safeguard the health of the heart.

Of course, you should take regular exercise of sufficient intensity to enhance the cardiovascular system.

Of course, you must change unhealthy eating habits as suggested in our Plan-21.

But, above all, you must identify and change your hostile cynical and mistrustful thoughts. As the noradrenaline hypothesis shows, such negative ideas and emotions can significantly damage your health.

Changing those ideas is the key to healthy longevity. When coming back from a heart attack, what you eat matters less than what's eating you.

INDEX

(References in **bold** refer to illustrations)

action 89, 90–91, 114–15
adrenaline 68, 70, 71–2, 74
alcohol 3, 34, 47, 172, 190–91, 194, 202
altering perspectives 89, 92, 129–32
amnesty 89, 92, 125–6
anger 53–4, 61–2, 63–5, 68, 113
   management 88, 92, 111, 127–9
   and noradrenaline 72–6
angina 18, 55, 68, 78
anticipation 89, 90, 111–14, 161
anxiety 8, 9, 12, 75, 114, **115**, 126, 214
   test 17
appraisal 89, 91, 118–24
arousal 64, 68–71, **72**, 73, 74, 83–4, 93, 115
arrhythmia 68, 77, 78
arteries, narrowing of 18–20, **19**, 52

assertiveness 89, 92, 111, 126–7
assisted relaxation 90, 92, 126, 134–69
   21-day programme 142–168
   preparation for 134–42
   see also relaxation
atheroma 18, 52, 68, 77–9
autonomic nervous system (ANS) 71, 88, 134, 141, 165, 212
avoidance 8, 10, 21, 89, 91, 114–15, 116–18
awareness 89, 90

beliefs 120–24
beta-blockers 24, 75, 217
blood pressure 3, 5, 30–31, 45–9, 82, 191, 212
burn-out stress syndrome (BOSS) 85–6

caffeine 73, 191–3, 202
calories 171, 172, 181, 190–91, 194, 203–5
carbohydrates 50, 176–9, 194, 199, 200–201

cardiac regulation 162
cardiovascular system,
    assessment of 30–32
cheeks 29, 43–4
cholesterol 20, 25, 49–50, 51,
    175, 181, 194
  level 3, 31–2, 82
clots, blood 18, 77
competition 60, 75, 210–11
constructive fantasy 112, 127,
    129, 155–7, 158, 159,
    163–4, 166, 167, 168
control, loss of 84, 113–14, **115**
coronary heart disease (CHD)
    17–18, 47, 50, 60

denial of reality 8, 10–11, 21,
    114–15
diet 47, 50, 194, 200
  21-point plan 194–208
  assessment of 32–4
dilemmas 121–3
drugs 24–5

emotions 11, 60, 78, 110
  assessment of 36–8
exercise 2–3, 36, 52–3, 209–19

family history 35, 51
fast food 33, 171, 173, 204
fat 20, 172, 179–82
  and fatty acids 77, 175, 180
  saturated 179–80, 194,
    201–2
fibre 183–7, 194, 198–9
fight or flight 68–71, 77
fish 175–6, 194, 198
fruit and vegetables 34, 184–7,
    194, 195–8, 199

Girth Test 26–7, 40

hand warming 165, 168
heart
  function of 14–17, **15**
  location of 13–14, **14**
homoeostasis 71, **74**, 81–3, 88
hostility 3, 53, 60, 61, 63–5,
    68–70, 75, 125
humourlessness 60, 66, 132–3
hurrying 60, 65–6
hypertension 47–9, 51, 190
hyperventilation 78, 140–41

jaw 29, 44

life goals 116–18, 132
lifestyle, changing 5–7, 23,
    170–72, 205–8
lipoproteins 76–7

massage, forehead 159, 160,
    162, 168
minerals 175, 184, 185, 188,
    195, 196, 197
mouth 28–30, 41–5

negative thoughts
  challenging 103–5, 106, 164
noradrenaline 66, 70–76, **75**,
    78, 88
nucleic acid 176, 185, 198

organically grown foods 187,
    194, 199

pain, chest 18, 21, **21**
peak performance stress level
    (PPSL) 83, 84, 85, 95, 113
perfectionism 124
personality 53, 55–68
  Type A 53, 55–60, 73, 77, 93
  Type B 53
  Type H 53, 60–66, 210–11

projection 8, 11–12
proteins 173–6
pulse rate 3, 82, 216–17
  carotid **22**, 23

recovery, barriers to 8–12
relaxation
  active 166–7
  and oral tension 44–5
  progressive 144–54, **147, 148**, 168
  rapid 161, 166, 168
  scale 143
  see also assisted relaxation
risk factor 3, 23–4, 25, 40–54, 56–66, 67–8, 78–9
  assessing 26–54
  chart **39**

salt 32–3, 47, 171, 186, 189–90, 194, 201
smoking 2, 3, 35, 49, 52, 141
snags 122–3
stress 44, 57, 113
  anniversary effect on 111
  chart 108–10
  and homoeostasis 81–3
  and ill health 86–88
  management 80–92
  management check-list 168–9
  responses **94**, 94–5, 96, 98–100, 107–8
  scale 105–6
stress diary 93–110
  analysing 100–101, 106
  purpose of 95, 110
  using 122, 125, 127, 163
sugar 33, 50, 171, 176–9, 200–201
symptoms of heart disease 20–23

tea and coffee 191–3, 194, 202
teeth 29–30, 44
Ten Commandments of stress management 89–90
thrombosis 18, 52, 78, 141
time management 65–6, 86–7, 129, 130, 131, 132
tongue **28**, 28, 42–3
traps 122, 123
triglyceride 3, **75**, 76, 174, 176

vitamins 175, 185, 186, 187–8, 194, 195, 196, 197, 207–8

walking 212–18
water 34, 50, 188–9, 194, 200
weight 2, 27–8, 40–41
work and heart disease 84–5, 86–7